Stuck between the Cootches.

I don't have a lot of experience with people calling me names. However, what I have learned from watching this kind of scene between other people is that the person who is being called a name can either go the "ignore it" route (also known as the Mommy Maneuver, because it's what moms always tell their kids to do), or they can intimidate their attacker with their superior wit.

"I don't believe we've been introduced," I began in what I hoped was a very superior and intimidating way. "I'm . . ."

"Let's keep it that way," Spike broke in. Then he called out to the room in general, "Are these seating arrangements permanent? Am I being punished? I haven't done anything yet, and you've put me in the front row. I am not a front-row type. Where are the cool guys sitting?" he yelled out as he knelt on his chair and surveyed the room. "Oh," he said in a lower tone. "There aren't any."

OTHER PUFFIN BOOKS YOU MAY ENJOY

A YEAR WITH
Butch AND Spike

Gail Gauthier

PUFFIN BOOKS

For RJ—just in case

PUFFIN BOOKS
Published by the Penguin Group
Penguin Putnam Books for Young Readers,
345 Hudson Street, New York, New York 10014, U.S.A.
Penguin Books Ltd, 27 Wrights Lane, London W8 5TZ, England
Penguin Books Australia Ltd, Ringwood, Victoria, Australia
Penguin Books Canada Ltd, 10 Alcorn Avenue, Toronto, Ontario, Canada M4V 3B2
Penguin Books (N.Z.) Ltd, 182-190 Wairau Road, Auckland 10, New Zealand

Penguin Books Ltd, Registered Offices: Harmondsworth, Middlesex, England

First published by G. P. Putnam's Sons,
a division of The Putnam & Grosset Group,1998
Published by Puffin Books,
a division of Penguin Putnam Books for Young Readers, 2000

3 5 7 9 10 8 6 4 2

THE LIBRARY OF CONGRESS HAS CATALOGED THE G. P. PUTNAM'S SONS EDITION AS FOLLOWS:
Gauthier, Gail, date A year with Butch and Spike / Gail Gauthier.
p. cm.
Summary: Upon entering sixth grade, straight-A student Jasper falls under
the spell of the dreaded, irrepressible Couture cousins.
[1. Schools—Fiction. 2. Humorous stories.] I. Title.
PZ7.G23435Yh 1998 [Fic]—dc21 97-13823 CIP AC
ISBN 0-399-23216-8

This edition ISBN 0-698-11827-8

Printed in the United States of America

Contents

One

Are These Seating Arrangements Permanent?

The Cootches.

They were all I could think of as I stood at the end of my driveway waiting for the school bus. I hadn't been able to get them off my mind since the day in June when I had heard that, for the first time ever, the Couture cousins would be placed in the same class for the following school year. Mine.

The Cootches.

They had been my research project for the summer. In July, I had studied them at the park as they stood in line by the ice-cream truck one afternoon, easily batting back anyone who tried to cut ahead of them. In August, I had hidden behind a *Sports Illustrated for Kids,* so I could spy on them as they prowled the adult fiction area in the public library, opening books and reading dirty sections aloud to each other before laughing and shelving them out of order. Just the week before school started, I had dropped a dozen eggs in the Stop and Shop parking lot

1

trying to catch one last glimpse of the van driving away with a My Kid Just Beat Up Your Honor Student bumper sticker on its rear fender and a Cootch in the front seat chugging soda from a two-liter bottle.

The Cootches.

My mom rubbed her cheek against mine, so we'd be close enough for my dad to get a first-day-of-school picture of the two of us. He has an entire film library of first-day-of-school pictures of me. You can see me growing taller and heavier each year but otherwise looking almost the same in every other way. I'm always a blue-eyed blond—my hair color never gets darker or lighter. Or longer or shorter, for that matter. My features are always right there on my face where they had been the year before. By the time you get to me in third or fourth grade you know pretty much what to expect.

"You're going to have a wonderful time at school this year," Mom said, just as she does every year.

And every year she's right.

My father started videotaping us, another one of those things that happens every year. Mom looked into the camera and said, "This is the first day of Jasper's last year at the Theodore Ervin Elementary School. He's going to be in sixth grade. His teacher is going to be Mrs. McNulty, who we know he is just going to love because he loves all his teachers. He's going to be a library aide, a Spanish tutor, a Teddy Scholar, and coeditor of the Teddy E. literary magazine!"

And the Cootches are going to be in my classroom! I added to myself as my parents began a long discussion about whether or not my father knew about the literary magazine. That led to another long talk about whether the celebration we had back in June was for my being appointed coeditor or for my getting perfect attendance or for my getting straight A's the last marking period.

All of which was captured forever on videotape.

We heard the bus turn onto our street and stop at a house around the corner.

The Cootches.

"You look so handsome in that new shirt," Mom said. "Doesn't he look handsome, John?"

"Love the shirt, Jasper," Dad called from behind his camera.

It was a blue knit shirt with a collar and three buttons at the neck, one of the kinds that have a tail that's a little longer in the back than in the front. My grandfather wore one just like it when he played golf. It was, I thought, a perfect first-day-of-school shirt.

The Cootches.

• • •

I could hear Donny Hall shouting to me as I made my way down the aisle of the crowded bus. I knew Donny from all the years we'd been playing baseball with the local league. But, then, everyone knew Donny from baseball.

"I heard at swimming lessons this summer that you're

going to be in Mrs. McNulty's class," Donny announced before I could drop down next to him. "I've got her, too. Do you suppose she'll rip up anyone's class work today? It *is* the first day of school, after all. That means there's no homework for her to throw away."

I could tell Donny had heard some of the stories that had been going around about Mrs. McNulty for . . . well, for all the time I'd been at Teddy E., anyway. I tried to reassure him.

"I'm sure that whatever Mrs. McNulty does, it will be for our own good."

Donny was not convinced. "She made Sam Taylor's older sister puke in class once. How was that for her own good?"

"She was going to be sick anyway," I pointed out.

"Yeah, but she would have done it in the girls' room if Mrs. McNulty had let her leave." Donny patted a pocket on his backpack. "I have some of those Ziploc food storage bags. I'm going to tape them under my table, so they'll be handy if I ever need them. She's not going to catch me."

If Theodore Ervin had had a speech department, Donny would have been its star pupil. He was the manliest-sounding kid at Teddy E. Even some of the male teachers sounded like women compared to Donny. He had grown six inches since the middle of the year before, and his voice had changed over President's Day weekend. When he said, "She's not going to catch me," shivers went right up my back.

"Mrs. McNulty has been the science fair advisor ever since we've been at Teddy E. I've known her since I entered the science fair for the first time back in kindergarten. She's . . ."

I had to think for a few seconds. It wasn't easy to come up with a word to describe Mrs. McNulty.

". . . okay. Sure. Mrs. McNulty is okay."

"So it's not true that she gives four tests a week and homework on weekends and vacations and makes kids memorize all the bones in the human body?"

I shrugged. "What's your point?"

"You ever see her at a baseball game? She comes once in a while. She yells at the umpires, the coaches, and the moms watching in the stands. She makes me nervous."

"She's always been nice to me. You've got nothing to worry about, Donny."

"Oh, sure she's nice to you," Donny complained. "Teachers are always nice to kids who like essay questions. Well," he sighed, "at least with Butch and Spike in our class I won't have to worry about getting in trouble much. They should keep Mrs. McNulty too busy to notice what I'm doing."

The Cootches.

"You think they'll be in trouble a lot?" I asked.

"Well, duh!"

"Have you been in class with them before? I played basketball with Butch one year, but he only was there for a few games because he broke his collarbone and had to quit."

Donny started to laugh. "I was in class with Butch in fourth grade. That was the year he and Spike got mad at those girls who formed a secret society they'd only let you join if you were a girl who could afford a herd of stuffed animals. Remember how the Cootches put cross-country ski wax on the toilets in the girls' room just before lunch one day because that was where they held their secret meetings?"

I did. "I would have liked to have seen that. Well, not really *seen* it," I quickly added. "I wouldn't have wanted to see girls, actually . . . you know . . . stuck . . . to toilets. It would have been interesting, though, to just stand outside the girls' room and listen to them yell."

"And I was in class with Spike just last year. I was there when he told Lyddy Daniels that the beard he'd brought for her to wear in the Walter Raleigh play was made out of hair he'd shaved off his neighbor's Irish setter's butt."

I'd heard about that, too. Lyddy had told us all about it at a Teddy Scholars' meeting one day when we were supposed to be enriching ourselves by writing haiku. We'd all agreed that it was a terrible thing. We also agreed we wished we could have seen her face when she found out.

"Well, she asked for it," Donny concluded. "She forced the other kids to let her play Sir Walter Raleigh. Whenever one of the Cootches does something to somebody you can pretty much figure they had it coming."

The Cootches.

• • •

When we arrived at school, who did we find leaning against a wall of lockers just outside our classroom door but Lyddy Daniels herself.

Lyddy looks a lot like a child actress. I don't mean she's beautiful or anything. I mean she looks like somebody who would be chosen to play a schoolgirl in a movie. She's tall and thin and has long blond hair and just a few freckles across the top of her nose. Some people think she's stuck on herself. I've seen a lot of Lyddy over the years because we're both in Teddy Scholars. If I try very hard, I am sometimes able to think of her as not stuck on herself at all, just misunderstood because she's so smart.

"What's the noise in there?" I asked her.

"It's Mrs. McNulty."

"What . . . what's she doing?" Donny asked. It was hard to believe that this was the same Donny Hall who could just approach home plate with a bat in his hand and send an entire outfield running.

"Talking."

The noise wasn't actually *all* that bad. It just sounded as if the bass had been turned up too loud on a stereo.

And Mrs. McNulty wasn't actually trying to be loud. She couldn't help herself. Large people often have large voices.

"Go on in," Lyddy urged me. "Hurry."

"What's the rush?" I asked.

"I'm trying to guess where everyone will be sitting so I can pick a place far away from Butch and Spike," she explained.

The Cootches.

"What a great idea!" Donny exclaimed. "I'm going to try to guess where they're sitting, so I can pick a spot right next to them. Just think how well behaved and smart I'll look if I'm sitting with the Cootches."

Lyddy looked at Donny for a moment as if she were considering that possibility. "I suppose it *might* help," she said doubtfully.

Well, I did go in, and I hurried, too. It was my first day in a new classroom, after all. How could I help but hurry? I loved school. I loved finding out who was in my class. I loved getting my new books. I loved ripping into the first assignment of the year.

And on top of all that, I was going to be in the same room with the Cootches.

"Keep those nameplates on the tables!"

That was the first thing I heard as I entered the room.

"I have to be able to figure out who you people are! You! At the door!" Mrs. McNulty shouted at someone behind me. "Come on in! You're at the right place!"

I looked over my shoulder to see a short, chunky, dark-haired girl cringing in the doorway. Her first name was Christine, I knew, because we had been in class together once before. At least, I *thought* we had been in class together. I couldn't remember actually ever having spoken to her. Or where she had sat. Or anything about her, for that matter. Was she the girl who had eaten the erasers off of everyone's pencils in first grade? I wondered as I watched her study the shelves full of faded dictionaries and stiff, musty *National Geographic*s. Could that have been Christine? Or was . . .

"I see you back there!" That statement was shot toward the back of the classroom. "What did I tell you? I told you to *leave the nameplates where they are*. You are starting the year seated in alphabetical order. Alphabetical order! It's the finest teaching tool ever devised. If that's the only thing you learn this year, I'll be satisfied."

Suddenly the tone of her voice changed, and the volume came down to a nearly normal level. "Jasper! It's so good to see you here." Mrs. McNulty beamed down at me. "I was delighted when I saw your name on my class list," she whispered, meaning her voice now carried only to the third row of tables. "It's going to be a wonderful year. I've been looking forward to it all summer. Here's your seat, dear."

Mrs. McNulty tapped one of the four tables at the front of the room with a fingernail she had painted to match the burgundy culottes she was wearing.

"But, Mrs. McNulty, my last name begins with G. I shouldn't be in the front row."

Not that I objected to being in the front row, of course. In fact, it was my favorite place to be.

"I want a boy of your abilities up front where you can inspire me," Mrs. McNulty explained with a smile and a wink. Then her head snapped up as something caught her eye.

"Hey!" she boomed. "No writing on those name-plates!"

"Jas-per! In-spire me-e-e-e!" Donny sang from the table behind me, where he'd found his nameplate.

I ignored him and slid onto my chair.

Each table in the classroom held two students. Lyddy was settling into the far seat at the table to my right. I thought it was too bad she hadn't been placed at my table. She was the perfect person to have sitting next to you. She never fooled around. She never talked when she wasn't supposed to. She always had her homework done on time, or even early, and she took good notes and kept her textbooks covered and her loose-leaf binder in perfect order. She . . .

"What are you doing in this row?" Lyddy suddenly demanded. "The G's shouldn't be in with the first letters of the alphabet. You are not supposed to be here."

"Mrs. McNulty told me to sit here. She said she wanted me in the front row," I explained. I tried to sound modest.

I was busy thinking of ways I might inspire Mrs. McNulty when I heard someone sit down next to me. Before I had a chance to look up, I heard a disgusted snort and then, "Well, *this* is different. Usually I'm placed next to a girl, because girls are *so* good and *such* good influences."

A Cootch. Right there, beside me.

I could feel my crew cut bristling . . . the hair on my arms, too.

A hand reached over, snapped my nameplate off the table, and took just a second to read it before slapping it facedown in front of me. "Oops! My mistake! I see I've been placed next to a girl again after all!"

Don't get me wrong. Girls are fine people. When I was in preschool, I even invited them to my birthday parties. There's absolutely nothing wrong with being called a girl—if you are one. If you're not . . . well, let's just say I knew what Spike Couture's very first words to me meant.

I don't have a lot of experience with people calling me names. However, what I have learned from watching this kind of scene between other people is that the person who is being called a name can either go the "ignore it" route (also known as the Mommy Maneuver, because it's what moms always tell their kids to do), or they can intimidate their attacker with their superior wit.

"I don't believe we've been introduced," I began in what I hoped was a very superior and intimidating way. "I'm . . ."

"Let's keep it that way," Spike broke in. Then he called out to the room in general, "Are these seating arrangements permanent? Am I being punished? I haven't done anything yet, and you've put me in the front row. I am *not* a front-row type. Where are the cool guys sitting?" he yelled out as he knelt on his chair and surveyed the room. "Oh," he said in a lower tone. "There aren't any."

"Hey! I'm a cool guy!" Donny objected.

Spike Couture! I'm sitting next to Spike Couture! I could hear myself screaming inside my own head as I stared into Spike's ear—the one with a small gold hoop through its lobe. I barely noticed when the seat to my right, the one across the aisle between Lyddy and me, was filled.

By Butch Couture.

"Jasper!" Butch actually sounded glad to see me. "I bet *you* brought paper. I need something to draw on." He leaned over, opened my new dark green notepad, and tore out a couple of sheets of paper. "Whoops! I ripped those. Give me another couple. And do you have one of those pencil pouches in that loose-leaf binder? I thought you would. Yeah, this oughtta hold me."

The Cootches. On either side of me instead of . . . somewhere else. Which is where I had always thought of them. All summer long when I had imagined what life in sixth grade would be like, I had always imagined the Cootches in a far corner, in another row . . . somewhere else.

I was having trouble breathing.

"You know this Jasper person, Butch?" Spike asked in amazement.

"Sure. We were on the same basketball team the year I broke my collarbone . . . or dislocated my shoulder . . . or fractured the bone in my leg. I know! It was the year I broke *Andy Negrelli's* leg. No, that was during soccer."

Spike broke in with another question. "Isn't this Jasper person supposed to be an awful grind?"

Butch looked a little vague, as if he didn't quite understand what his cousin had asked him.

"The word 'grind' has several meanings," I—the Jasper person—explained, still hoping to intimidate the Cootches, this time with my superior knowledge of vocabulary. "In this case he's using it as a noun so it means 'a person who studies seriously.' "

"Or it could mean 'an obnoxious or annoying person,' " Lyddy broke in.

Lyddy also has a superior knowledge of vocabulary.

Butch leaned forward so he could see his cousin and said, "Yes."

"You can sit next to me, Spike," Donny offered. "I'm not a good student or obnoxious, either."

Spike liked that idea a lot.

"We can't do that," I said as Spike jumped up and signaled for Christine, who had been placed at Donny's table, to trade places with him.

"It's almost done."

"We can't!" I insisted. "We were assigned to these seats. We were *told* where to sit. We can't just get up and move . . . no matter how much we'd like to."

Spike's brown eyes popped. "And what is that supposed to mean?"

"N . . . nothing," I replied.

"I don't think he likes you, Spike," Butch said.

Spike didn't look as if he were bothered much by the prospect of me or anyone else not liking him.

"What is going on up there?" Mrs. McNulty asked as she headed toward the front of the room. "You two up front . . . Spike and Butch. Stop that immediately."

"Stop what?" Butch objected.

"He started it," Spike said, pointing at me.

Mrs. McNulty patted me on the head as she walked toward the front of the room. "Don't even think of using that argument. I've known Jasper for years. There's not a calmer, more responsible child in the sixth grade."

Spike whispered, "Calm this," and thumbed his nose at me. It was one of those double jobs—one hand in front of the other and both hands in front of the nose.

I was having a hard time feeling my arms and legs, and my stomach seemed to be gone, too. I tried to concentrate on Mrs. McNulty, who was writing "Middle School" on the chalkboard at the front of the room.

"Your biggest job this year is to prepare for next year," she announced to the class. "We have to get you in shape for middle school. Now, make no mistake. They call it a middle school, but it's a junior high school. They're not kidding anybody with their little name change. Next year you'll be running from class to class *all day long*. There'll be no more baby-sitting! There'll be twenty or thirty minutes of homework in *every* class, *every* night."

Well, that was something good to look forward to, I thought as I tried to keep one eye on each of the Cootches.

"The halls in the middle school will be crowded. Mobbed in all likelihood. Most days you won't even have time to force your way back to your locker between classes. And you'd better make darn sure you go to the bathroom before you leave home. Even if they let you into one of the rest rooms during the three minutes you're allowed to get from one class to another, you won't want to use them because there won't be any doors on the stalls. They take them off to keep kids from . . . smoking."

Butch and Spike gasped in unison.

Mrs. McNulty smiled at Christine, who was still cringing over this little stack of pastel paperbacks she had piled on her table. "You don't have to worry about middle school, because I won't let you leave my class until I know you're ready to go."

"That makes me feel a whole lot better," Spike sneered under his breath.

Butch had his arm, the one with a little bit of ratty old cast on the end of it, up in the air.

"Yes?"

"I'm ready to go now, Mrs. McNulty."

"I will be the judge of that."

There was a knock at the door. It opened and there was—

"Ms. Spendolini."

Our new principal's name rippled across the classroom as each student there eagerly greeted her. The boys did, anyway.

Ms. Spendolini was as small as Mrs. McNulty was big. She was short, anyway. In places her figure was what my mother describes as generous, and she often wore belts around her tiny waist that just made the generous parts look more generous. While Mrs. McNulty's hair was always short, its color varied from year to year—sometimes from month to month. Ms. Spendolini's hair was long and always the same shade of brown. Mrs. McNulty's face was kind of puffy, which probably explained why her eyes looked small and her mouth looked as if she didn't have any lips. But Ms. Spendolini's eyes were huge and dark and her mouth . . . Well, I don't know how to describe Ms. Spendolini's mouth, but I think all women's mouths should look like it.

That had been my humble opinion, anyway, since Ms. Spendolini had joined the Teddy E. staff the year before.

"Ms. Spendolini!" Spike called out louder than anyone else. "Come on in."

"I'm sorry to interrupt you, Mrs. McNulty, but I wanted to let Jasper and Lyddy know that I'm going to be the literary magazine advisor this year," Ms. Spendolini explained. "Mrs. Casabian usually does it, but she's going on maternity leave in December. I was editor of my school newspaper when I was in sixth grade. I loved it. So, I thought this sounded like a job for me."

I thought it sounded like a job for her, too.

The Cootches.

"Ms. Spendolini, could you . . ."

"Raise your hand, Spike," Mrs. McNulty ordered.

Spike raised one of his hands off the table, but he didn't look as if he liked doing it.

"Since you're going to be the advisor, could you please do something about how boring the literary magazine is? I've never been able to read more than the first page."

"No. Why don't *you* do something about how boring the literary magazine is, Spike? You have the good luck to be in class with Lyddy and Jasper. Tell them your ideas. The three of you should put your heads together and see what you can do."

My breathing problem was back. From the looks of Lyddy's face, her lungs weren't doing their best for her, either.

"You mean I could be coeditor with them?" Spike asked.

"That would probably be too many editors," Ms. Spendolini replied.

"How about assistant editor?"

"I'm not talking about anything that formal. Why don't you write something for the literary magazine—something that's not boring, of course," Ms. Spendolini suggested. "Anyone can make suggestions to the editors, you know. And, Butch? We need artwork. How about if you go to work for us, too? The magazine doesn't come out until May, and the editorial work doesn't begin until after Christmas, so there's plenty of time."

"I don't know. I've never done anything for the literary magazine before."

There were encouraging murmurs in the room, and a few "Come on, Spike"s from the back.

Ms. Spendolini smiled. "The people are speaking, Spike. They want you."

"Well, in that case, I might be able to find some time in my busy schedule to come up with a few ideas."

Ms. Spendolini led the class in a round of applause and smiled down at Spike while I just sat there with my tongue drying out because my mouth was hanging open. It's as if she likes him, I thought. It's as if he were the one who had perfect attendance last year. It's as if he were the one who nearly had straight A pluses twice. It's as if . . .

"Silence!"

The class became so quiet that we were able to hear a "What was that?" coming out of the next room.

"Ms. Spendolini is still new here," Mrs. McNulty said. She smiled at Ms. Spendolini in a way I wouldn't have wanted anyone to smile at me. "I don't think she realizes just how carefully I run my classroom," she said.

Her tone of voice suggested that Ms. Spendolini better understand that soon.

"You know, Mrs. McNulty, I think you're 100 percent correct. I *don't* know how you run your classroom. But I'd like to. I thought I'd drop by a few times this fall just to see how you manage things. I'm really looking forward to it."

"I'm sure you'll be pleased," Mrs. McNulty said without ever wiping that creepy smile off her face.

"I'm so glad," Ms. Spendolini replied.

I could see Butch and Spike staring at both women, their heads turning from one to the other, as if they were totally absorbed in watching a very slow tennis match. They both looked disappointed when Ms. Spendolini winked (at me! I'm sure she was winking at me!) and said she had to be off to bother other teachers.

"Now, where were we?" Mrs. McNulty asked when we were alone again.

"On planet Earth, Mrs. McN. It's the blue planet with an atmosphere. Does that jog your mem—"

"Okay, you two," Mrs. McNulty growled. "Let's get one thing straight. You are *mine* . . . *MINE* . . . for the entire year. Don't think you're going to snow me like you've snowed some of these other so-called teachers in this school by being clever and smart. That kind of thing doesn't impress me."

"Clever? Smart?" Butch repeated. "Spike! I think she likes us!"

"Butch, your career as a clown is over as of this minute. You two have spent five years in this school, doing just about whatever you wanted. Well, that is over. And it's over because I'm going to stop it, and I'm stopping it *now*."

Spike looked Mrs. McNulty in the eye and said, "Six years."

"What's that?"

"Six years. We've spent six years in this school, doing just about whatever we wanted. You forgot about kindergarten."

The Cootches.

I hoped the feeling in my legs would come back in time for me to get on the bus to go home.

• • •

We spent the rest of the morning trying out our new hall lockers, taping our names to our storage cubbies, and going over Mrs. McNulty's discipline system, which covered classroom behavior, homework, playground activity, rude talk, overdue library books, personal hygiene, proper dress, appropriate bedtimes, and good nutrition.

At lunch Butch laughed and said, "It's going to take Mrs. McNutty the rest of the week to get through all that stuff."

"How would you know? You slept through most of it,"

Lyddy complained. "I'd better not ever find drool on my side of the table."

"Look at her," Spike said suddenly. He was scowling toward the other end of the cafeteria where Mrs. McNulty had just directed two first-graders to take their chairs into a corner and face the wall. "She isn't even on lunch duty today. She's just here 'cause she's mean." He sat slouched next to me with the one-pound bag of barbecue potato chips he'd brought for lunch propped open on his chest.

Personally, I thought Mrs. McNulty had come to the cafeteria to make sure we sat in alphabetical order at the table she had assigned us.

"I'd be mean, too, if I'd been stuck with both of you for an entire school year," Lyddy complained. "But then I *am* stuck with you, aren't I?"

"And you *are* mean, too," Butch told her.

Lyddy was sitting right next to Butch, and she was able to get right into his face—a whole lot closer than I would have thought she'd want to get. "You'll find out what mean is if you wreck my chances at winning one of those sixth-grade academic awards next spring. They're competitive. I have to beat out every other kid in the sixth grade to get one. I have a good chance of winning the Theodore Ervin Memorial Award for Excellence in Math and the Theodore Ervin Memorial Award for Excellence in Science and . . . oh, heck, I have a good chance at winning all of them. But I could lose every-thing to Kimberly Stafford in Ms. Napolitano's room if Mrs. McNulty has to waste too much of our class time on you two."

"Don't worry, Lyddy," Spike assured her. "I've heard you're sure to win the Theodore Ervin Memorial Award for Biggest Pain in the Butt. No one else can touch you in that category."

Butch nodded soberly in agreement while everyone else at the table roared.

I sat there feeling as if I'd been expecting to watch a disaster movie and instead found myself in it.

The Cootches.

Two

My Wonderful Year

There is something scary about the Cootches when they are together, which, because I was sitting between them, was how I always saw them. I'm not talking about Spike's pierced ear, though that was scary, too. There's just something about them that is so . . . alike. They both have brown curly hair, but that isn't it because Spike wears his a lot longer than Butch does and his curls aren't quite so tight. Their eyes are sort of a chocolate color, and they both have these wide mouths that ought to make them look like frogs but don't because their faces are so broad. Spike's face is all cheekbone, though, while Butch's is squarer, meatier looking. In fact, everything about Butch is square and meaty while Spike has a scarecrowish aspect to him.

No, what really marks the Cootches as being connected somehow isn't so much the way they look when you're looking at *them* as the way they look when they're looking at *you*. You see it mostly around their eyes, but it's there around their mouths, too. It's that expression you see on kids in grocery shopping carts and deer caught in headlights. The Cootches always seem as if they've just seen something that startled and amazed them. And when they're together they often turn to each other with that look on their faces and you know that they've just had the same thought at the same time. At that point, you can bet that more likely than not one or the other of them is going to do something about it.

By the beginning of the second week of school I'd had all I could take of them and asked Mrs. McNulty if I could move my seat.

She was filing her fingernails over the trash can, a little job she tended to first thing every morning while the classroom monitors were cleaning the chalkboards, taking attendance, and collecting homework. She looked up at me just long enough to say no, and then went back to work.

I was surprised.

"It's not as if I'm actually supposed to be there, Mrs. McNulty. It's not alphabetical for me to be there."

"I've made a special allowance for you, Jasper, dear," she replied.

Special?

"You may not have noticed, Mrs. McNulty, but Butch and Spike talk all the time. Since I sit between them and they can't talk to each other they keep talking to me. They have something to say about everything. And then

you know Butch, well, he . . . burps. And he's always borrowing things, only it's not really borrowing since he
never gives anything back. Spike . . ."

Mrs. McNulty looked up at me again and smiled.
When she's into a serious smile, her eyes almost disappear.

"*They* do those things, dear. *You* don't. That's why I
placed you between them. You're their role model. You're
a role model for every child in the school. Didn't you
know that?"

"Really?"

"Of course, you are." She lowered her voice. "I
wouldn't be at all surprised if next spring you're elected
Student of the Year."

I thought that was a possibility, too. But to hear a
teacher say it!

Mrs. McNulty patted my arm. "You're my secret
weapon. Now, why don't you go sit down. We'll be ready
to start soon."

My self-esteem was really cooking as I headed back to
my desk. Unfortunately, it boiled away when Butch
stretched across the space between his table and mine,
leaned his head on my shoulder, and let out a belch that
had to have been heard in the next classroom.

"Oh, no," he groaned as he rubbed his chest. "I think
I hurt myself."

"Then you shouldn't have done it," I said.

Spike leaned across our table (and me) toward his

cousin. "I guess Mrs. McNulty's secret weapon told you."

Butch trembled and made his teeth chatter so that his braces, which almost always needed to have something tightened, seemed to rattle in his head.

"Some of us just don't understand what's so funny about burping," I snapped.

"That might make a good story for the literary magazine," Spike said thoughtfully. " 'What's So Funny About Burping?' Yeah. I'd like to see that."

"Nothing. There is *nothing* funny about burping."

Butch shook his head sadly. "You're hopeless."

"He's not hopeless, Butch, he's a role model. You know—one of those kids who always does what the teachers want them to do. Then the teachers point at them and tell everybody how wonderful they are, so we'll all want to be like them."

"Except we don't," Butch pointed out.

"You know that and I know that, but the role models don't know that," Spike explained.

Butch said, "The teachers must pick the slow kids for that job. Ya think?"

I flipped open my green notebook, hoping I could bring the conversation to an end if I could somehow make myself look too busy to notice them. There, on the inside cover, I found an elaborate web filled with spiders with perfect little human faces. It totally covered the area where I usually kept track of my test scores.

"I did that," Butch said modestly. "Save it. It will be worth money someday."

"I'm about to assign the year's first writing assignment," Mrs. McNulty roared. "Are you ready? You are to observe a natural phenomenon and write a two-page paper describing it. I want your papers at a quarter to nine tomorrow morning. Spelling counts. Please don't bore me."

There were two groans, a gasp, several sighs, and someone called out, "Is TV natural?"

"Did I give you the impression that I was finished? I'm sorry. Each page is to include one metaphor—no more, no less. This is a test of your ability to follow instructions. Following instructions! After alphabetical order it's the most important thing you'll learn this year. Now, who wants to tell me what a metaphor is?"

I got my right arm up just a second before Lyddy's.

"A metaphor," I said, "is a way of describing something by comparing it to something totally different."

"Exactly." Mrs. McNulty smiled and nodded at me. "An example of a metaphor might be . . . oh, let's say 'Her eyes were like two pools of pure, clean water.' Now, what am I actually saying? Yes, Lyddy?"

"That her eyes were blue."

"Exactly. Now . . . Yes, Spike?"

"Like"? I thought. "Like two pools of pure, clean water"?

Spike finished a yawn and said, "Two things, Mrs.

27

McN. First, I think everyone should understand that there is no such thing as a bad writing assignment. There are only bad writers."

Mrs. McNulty dropped a piece of chalk, and I thought again, "Like"?

"And, second, 'Her eyes were like two pools of pure, clean water' isn't actually a metaphor. It's a simile. A metaphor doesn't use the words 'like' or 'as.' A metaphor would be something like, oh, 'She was a wolf, pacing before them, selecting her prey.' 'She looked like a wolf pacing before them, selecting her prey' is a simile. I like metaphors better myself. You have to think about them more."

Another person . . . say, me, for instance . . . might have gone silent at the sight of Mrs. McNulty's face. It had taken on the tight, stony look of those statues that guard Egyptian tombs—the ones that wipe out entire archaeological parties because they went one step too far into the sacred chamber. But Spike just rambled on, cranking out every metaphor or simile he could think of.

"Thank you, Spike," Mrs. McNulty said twice.

The first time, Spike said, "You're welcome," and kept right on going. The second time, he came back with, "Oh, I just thought of another . . ."

"You've thought of quite enough."

"No, no, this is a good one! I can't remember it exactly, but you know that guy who wrote the *Soup* books?

He wrote a poem that compared autumn to some fancy dress dance. The whole poem was like that. And at the end? When November came? The dance was over." Spike turned around so he could face the students. "And that, class," he concluded, "is what's known as an extended metaphor."

"I'll take over now."

"Sure. If you think you can."

Mrs. McNulty silently pointed to the door.

"You want me to leave?" Spike asked in amazement. "Is that my reward for correcting your embarrassing mistake and making sure you didn't . . ."

"Yes. And take a chair with you. I have a feeling you're going to be out there a lot today."

Butch's arm flew up.

"Can I go, too?"

• • •

In the next few weeks, Butch and Spike spent a lot of time out in the hallway.

When Mrs. McNulty announced the location of the fall field trip, Butch exclaimed, "The Tarbutt Homestead! That dead old fart's house! We're always going to places like that. Can't we go someplace that doesn't stink?"

"The science museum we went to in third grade didn't actually stink," Spike recalled. "That was when my mother was banned forever from serving as a field trip chaperone because she fell asleep during the planetarium show. Really, it was a good trip."

"Speaking of planetariums, my father told me this great Uranus joke. 'Why is the . . .' "

They were out in the hall before Butch could deliver his punch line.

Then there was the time Mrs. McNulty assigned a book report and Spike said, "I don't want to read *Lassie Come Home*. Lassie is out in the wilderness and what does she do? She goes home. How lame can you get? If I were going to do a book report (and I'm not saying I am), I would do it on *Call of the Wild*. When the dog in that story found himself out in the wilderness, he ran with wolves."

"Yeah, Buck's a cool dog," Butch agreed.

"Of course, Buck's a boy dog so he can't help but be cooler than Lassie, who is a girl," Spike declared.

Someone (a girl, according to Spike) began throwing pencils, there was some shouting, and by the time the uproar had died down, both Butch and Spike were out in the hall.

"You call this a vocabulary list?" Spike objected another day when Mrs. McNulty gave us our first list of the year. " *Ability? Congenial? Mirth?* When was the last time anyone here used the word *mirth?* Why can't we study some words we might actually use in our lifetimes? How about *horrendous?* Or *vile?* Or *retch?* *Retch* would be a good vocabulary word. And *stench.* I like *stench*, too."

Mrs. McNulty said he could like it just as well out in the hallway.

At lunch Donny said, "I wish I could have spent the last two hours sitting in the hall."

"Anybody can get kicked out of class," Spike pointed out.

"Yeah. It's not like you have to be a genius or something to do it," Butch added. He looked at me and grinned. "It's not like you have to be a Teddy Scholar and take some kind of special class on finding your way into the hall."

Donny shook his head. "I just don't think I have what it takes to manage it."

"What about making your own vocab list?" Spike asked. "Do you have what it takes to manage that?"

Evidently Donny did, because he and the Cootches went to work preparing a lengthy list of the words they'd like to see on their fantasy vocabulary test, most of which came out of the category Mrs. McNulty referred to as Rude Talk.

"Come on, you guys," I said as I nervously eyed Mrs. McNulty and the other two teachers who had lunch duty that day. "Someone might hear you."

"And why is that a problem?" Butch asked.

"It's not actually a problem. It's just that I put all my books in my locker and now I've finished reading this one so I don't have anything to do for the rest of the period. I'll have to . . . I'll have to just sit here, I guess."

There was a pause while everyone zoomed in on Christine Janicki, whose seat was next to Donny's, just as it was in the classroom. Her pale face flushed. "I interrupted someone, didn't I? I'm sorry. I was reading so I wasn't paying attention. I thought someone was speaking to me. I . . . I . . ."

It was the first time Christine had said more than an occasional "Pass these papers to the end of the row" to any of us, and her attempt at speech wasn't going well. She was embarrassed, and no one likes embarrassment. The correct thing to do was to pretend we didn't notice that she hadn't been able to follow our conversation, and that's what we set to work to do.

Most of us, anyway.

"Interrupting people is no big deal," Butch said, as if he'd given the matter a lot of thought and come to that conclusion. "It's not like getting caught with your finger up your nose or something. Of course, that's no big deal, either." He pointed to a couple of cold, hard French fries left on Christine's tray. "You going to eat those?"

Christine shook her head, and Butch helped himself to her fries as well as those of several other people who had suddenly lost their appetites.

"You know," Donny said to Christine, "all the other teachers give locker passes during lunch period. If Mrs. McNulty wasn't in the cafeteria today, you'd be able to get one."

Spike tossed the remains of the day-old pizza he'd

brought for lunch onto my tray so I'd have to dispose of it. "You can get one even though she is here. Ask one of the other teachers. She can't keep them from giving you one."

Christine stared at him with her mouth open. At first I thought she was just terrified at the thought of going behind Mrs. McNulty's back. But she must have just been confused by how quickly she had become the center of attention because she said, "Oh, no. I don't want to get any of the teachers in trouble with Mrs. McNulty."

"They can't get in trouble for giving you a pass." Lyddy laughed.

Christine looked at Lyddy as if she were sizing her up, and Lyddy wasn't doing as well as Christine had expected. "Don't you know? The other teachers are afraid of Mrs. McNulty. You can tell by the way they all pretend to be doing something whenever she gets near them."

We all stretched and turned until we found Mrs. McNulty over by the trash cans. Sure enough, the only teacher near her was pretending to walk away . . . fast.

"Maybe the other teachers are smarter than we thought," Butch suggested.

I looked around the room. "Sometimes Ms. Spendolini comes into the cafeteria."

Spike turned his amazed Cootch look on me. "That's right! I bet she'd give Christine a pass. She's not afraid of the McNutt."

"Just forget about it. It's almost time for recess anyway. I'll skim the good parts of this book over again until they let us go."

"Reading at the table is unbelievably rude," Lyddy pointed out, which could have caused another embarrassment problem, and we'd only just managed to deal with the last one.

"Everything that's good to do is rude," Spike complained.

Donny bent to look at the cover of Christine's book. *"Pioneer Princess,"* he read aloud. "Gee, maybe you can use this for one of those book reports Mrs. McNulty's been talking about."

"Oh, come on, Donny. Christine's not going to find *that* on any reading list," Lyddy sneered.

"If it's not on a reading list, it's got to be good. What's it about?" Butch asked.

Christine's face, which was kind of small for someone her size, lit up. "It's all about the adventures of this beautiful thirteen-year-old pioneer girl who has to take care of her ten younger brothers and sisters during a blizzard *and* Indian attack while her father takes her mother east to see a doctor," she explained. "I don't have ten younger brothers and sisters, just three. But they seem like ten."

"Hmmm," Butch grunted. "Does anybody die? Get seriously injured? In the book, I mean."

"Do the Indians capture the girl and raise her as one of their own?" Spike asked hopefully.

"No, no, no! The girl saves everybody and brings peace to the plains!" Christine exclaimed.

Lyddy grudgingly admitted that she liked books with girls who save everyone. "But unless it's been approved by the sixth-grade teachers she's wasted her time reading it. I always pick my books from a reading list or get them approved before I read them."

"It's lunchtime!" Spike pointed out. "I, for one, never read anything approved by a teacher while I eat."

"Oh, come on, Spike. You never read anything approved by a teacher at all," his cousin told him.

"I would if they approved anything decent."

"I've heard that some of the teachers don't have reading lists," Christine said in a low voice, as if she were telling a horrible secret. "They let everyone read whatever they want to."

There was a lot of wistful sighing and head shaking over that information.

"Well," Lyddy said as she got ready to take her empty tray back to the kitchen, "it doesn't matter what other teachers do. The sixth-grade teachers have a reading list. If we want to see an A next to the word 'reading' on our report cards, we'll do our book reports on books from Mrs. McNulty's list. And I am going to see an A there. That's how you win awards, remember. You collect A's. You can be sure Kimberly Stafford isn't reading books that aren't on the list."

"If Kimberly Stafford jumped off a bridge, would you jump off a bridge?" Butch asked.

Lyddy smiled. "If there was an award for it, I would."

• • •

Things had been going quite well for me that particular day. First thing that morning Lyddy and I had worked on our Art from Recycled Materials project at Teddy Scholars, Spike was sent to the hall soon after we got back, and I knew we were starting a social studies unit on state and town history in the afternoon. Maybe my wonderful year will be starting sometime soon, I thought when we got back from lunch.

Then we were assigned to work groups.

"Why? Why, why, why do we have to work in a group?" Spike demanded.

Mrs. McNulty smiled a wide, skinny smile. "Because Ms. Spendolini says we have to, and we might as well get started with these town of West Adams projects."

"And do you do everything Ms. Spendolini tells you to, Mrs. McN.?" Butch asked.

Mrs. McNulty had been looking at her class list. Her head came up, and she gave Butch a strange look. "Of course, I do. And if you expect to get out of sixth grade, you will, too."

Spike looked at Butch and snorted. "I guess we'll be here a while."

There were twenty-four of us in the class, and Mrs. McNulty began to break us into groups of six. By now

36

there was no doubt, of course, of whose group I would be in.

"Lyddy and Jasper, you'll work with Butch and Spike."

Lyddy covered her face with her hands while Spike pounded the table with his fists. Mrs. McNulty looked out over the students, trying to find two more sacrifices.

"Oh! Oh! Mrs. McNulty! I'll work with Butch and Spike! Pick me!"

"Okay, Donny. You're in Group Three. Now, let's see . . ."

"Can we have Chrissie in our group?" Butch asked.

"Chrissie?"

We all looked around. There was no Chrissie in our class.

"Me. I think he means me," Christine said nervously. She may have just been worried that she'd misunderstood the conversation the way she had at lunchtime and was going to make a fool of herself by speaking up, though the prospect of having to work with the Cootches was enough to cause nervousness in most people.

"Yeah. Can we have her?" Butch asked Mrs. McNulty.

Mrs. McNulty just shrugged and went on.

Lyddy looked over at me and mouthed the words "Donny and Christine?" Then her arm shot up into the air and she waited patiently for Mrs. McNulty to finish what she was doing and notice her.

"Mrs. McNulty? I don't want to do anything to ruin

37

your plans for these work groups, but I was wondering if I could put in an early request for next time? The next time we have to do a group project could I work with Megan and—"

"There's not going to be a next time," Mrs. McNulty broke in.

"We only have to do it once?" Lyddy asked hopefully. "I thought—"

"I've divided this class into groups. My job is done. Make a decision and stick with it, class. It's a great time-saver. Remember my words."

"What exactly are you talking about?" Spike asked before I could get my hand up in the air to ask something similar.

"I mean you will be working in these groups for the entire year. Any time you have group projects, any time you go to the computer lab, any time you go on a field trip you will be in these groups. No thinking involved. Just do it.

"Now, who can tell me why Jonathan Tarbutt is an important historical figure?"

Spike and I turned to each other and for once *we* had the same thought at the same time. And the thought was . . .

Field trips?

Three

Something
to Think About

I am Mrs. Ezekial Tarbutt, and I am beginning my long day as a farmwife and mother to twelve children and aunt to Jonathan Tarbutt, the Revolutionary War hero you've come here to learn about."

Some people think of field trips as a day off from school. There's no such thing. One way or another, any day you spend away from the classroom comes back to haunt you. Field trips are no different. Either you're expected to write a paper on what you learned, or you have to write a letter to somebody thanking them for the swell time you had, or you have to work on some project or another at home because you couldn't use your free period at school because you weren't *at* school, you were *on* a field trip.

And then, of course, there are your classmates to deal with.

I started my day at the Tarbutt Homestead with Group Three listening to this woman who *clearly* could not be

39

Mrs. Ezekial Tarbutt because Mrs. Ezekial Tarbutt had been dead for nearly two hundred years. But you often see people at historic sites pretending to be dead people. Visitors are expected to go along with it. Usually I don't mind, but we were having an unusually hot autumn, and that particular day in early October was the tenth day in a row of ninety-degrees-plus temperatures. For just a moment I wished Mrs. Tarbutt would begin her day by turning on a fan instead of stoking the fire in her kitchen. But, of course, that would ruin this important historical experience.

"I will spend the biggest part of my day just providing food for my family of fourteen and whoever may visit us, such as Jonathan Tarbutt, the Revolutionary War hero," Mrs. Tarbutt told us. "You see how I am dressed in a long cotton gown with a long cotton slip under it? I have to be very careful as I work in my kitchen because it's not unusual for women in my day to get too close to the flames they're cooking over and set themselves on fire."

Butch and Spike exchanged a look, and suddenly I began to wonder if there was a twentieth-century fire extinguisher hidden in one of the antique cupboards.

"In addition to feeding my children and making their clothing, I also act as doctor to my large family. We don't have a telephone or neighbors and we live a long way from town, so contacting a doctor is done only for a very serious emergency."

"Like what?"

"I beg your pardon?" Mrs. Tarbutt said.

"What would be a big enough emergency to make it worthwhile to contact a doctor?"

"Oh, uh, if one of the children—or Jonathan Tarbutt, the Revolutionary War hero—had a very high fever that I couldn't bring down myself, we might contact the doctor. I might contact him if someone had broken a limb."

"What about amputations? Would you try to amputate one of the kids' legs yourself?"

"No, I don't believe I'd try to do that myself."

"Butch!" Mrs. McNulty snapped from her spot next to the fire. "Raise your hand before you ask a question! That's good museum manners."

Mrs. Tarbutt continued. "I would, however, have a number of remedies on hand because with twelve children—and visiting nephews—there would always be someone injuring themselves or getting sick." She picked up a bowl and held it out for us to look at. "I keep pieces of cotton like these handy, and when my children have an earache I put a little oil on them and put them into the children's ears. I always keep ginger so I can make poultices like these when my children have toothaches . . ."

Mrs. Tarbutt noticed Butch's hand waving wildly in the air. "Yes?"

"Do you have any leeches? You know, bloodsuckers for sucking blood out of people?"

"N . . . nooo. That's something a doctor would do. Perhaps it would be best if we switch to a little sewing project," Mrs. Tarbutt suggested.

"Shoot," Spike whispered to me. "I wanted to hear more about the things she stuck in little kids' ears and mouths."

"Do you mind?" Lyddy hissed at him.

"Can anyone tell me what a tussy-mussy is?" Mrs. Tarbutt asked.

Mrs. Tarbutt looked right over my upraised hand, as well as Lyddy's, and chose Christine.

"Me? She chose me?" Christine asked without lowering her arm.

"You did raise your hand," Donny reminded her.

"Oh, um. What was it? Oh, yes. A tussy-mussy is a thing that smells good that ladies in books hold up to their noses when there is something near them that smells bad."

Then she shrugged her shoulders as if she'd just passed on some common knowledge that everyone was expected to know.

"Exactly. Unfortunately, in the times when I, Mrs. Tarbutt, live, people don't bathe very frequently. And if I am in a closed-in place—say, church, or a public meeting of some sort—where there are a great many people, and it is winter and everyone is wearing their heavy woolen clothing or it is summer and it is very hot—"

"People will STINK!" Butch howled.

Spike raised his hand and waited until he was called

upon to speak. Then in an incredibly polite voice he said, "What do you mean when you say they didn't bathe very frequently? Just how often did they bathe?"

"It's hard to say, of course. My sons will bathe in the brook behind the house in the summer, but, of course, my daughters can't do that. It's not acceptable for young women to be seen in their underwear," Mrs. Tarbutt explained delicately.

"That hardly seems fair," Spike complained. "I guess they didn't have any equal rights laws back then, huh?"

"They had to swim in their underwear in colonial times?" I asked. "That must have been uncomfortable."

"In all the books I've read the guys swam naked," Christine said. "I don't think they had bathing suits."

"Naked!" Butch and Spike exclaimed.

"And the brook was behind this house?" Spike asked.

"It's still there," Mrs. Tarbutt replied.

"Change the subject, boys," Mrs. McNulty warned.

"Okay. I have a question about Jonathan Tarbutt," Butch admitted. "He must have stunk, huh, if he didn't take baths?"

Mrs. Tarbutt tried several times to reply to that before she was finally saved by Donny, who had raised his hand. "Oh, I think I'll take a question from this young man," she said. "He hasn't asked anything yet."

"Well, Mrs. Tarbutt, all those British people who lived back then and wore all those fancy clothes and white wigs—did they stink, too, or was it just us Americans?"

"Oh, you look so hot!" was how we were greeted by the curator at our next stop in the house. Unlike the woman who had claimed to be Mrs. Ezekial Tarbutt, this one was dressed in pink plaid Bermuda shorts and a yellow sleeveless tank top. It wasn't a historically accurate outfit, and it made the woman wearing it look as big as a house.

"You know, two hundred years ago, when Jonathan Tarbutt, the Revolutionary War hero's, aunt and uncle lived in this house," she began, "there were no fans and no air-conditioning. On top of that, the women all had to dress like Mrs. Tarbutt, the lady in the kitchen. And the men wore long sleeves and long pants year-round. They often wore wool year-round, too."

"Did they have deodorant back then?" Butch asked.

"You know, I've often wondered about that myself. Come on over here, I'm going to take you upstairs so we can see a bedroom."

"Listen," Butch warned his classmates, "any minute now people are going to start fainting from the heat. And when they do, we have to be careful to have them lie down so their blood can circulate to their brains."

"Anyone who faints will have more than their circulation to worry about when we get back in the classroom," Mrs. McNulty hissed.

"Now this room is furnished exactly the way a bedroom would have been furnished at the time Jonathan

Tarbutt, the Revolutionary War hero, lived. Do you see how lumpy the bed is? That's because it's filled with straw. They didn't have mattresses like we do. Did the lady in the kitchen tell you about how often people bathed back then?"

"She didn't tell us *exactly* how often," Spike answered.

"But she told you it wasn't often. You want to hear something else that's gross?" the curator asked confidentially.

Butch and Spike immediately agreed that they did, and that was all the encouragement the curator needed.

"Oh, I'm so glad because the next thing I'm going to tell you *is* gross. People back then didn't bathe very often, so they were dirty. Then, they slept on mattresses filled with straw, which they didn't clean very often. So . . . people back then were covered with flea and bedbug bites."

Christine and Lyddy squealed, but anybody could tell they were just being polite.

"I've heard grosser stuff," Butch said.

"Okay. I'll try again. There's only one thing in this room that actually belonged to Jonathan Tarbutt, the Revolutionary War hero's, aunt and uncle. Can anyone guess what it is?"

Some people guessed the bed or the stand next to the bed or the curling iron propped up next to the fireplace or the bed warmer or the clock on the mantel.

"What about that big casserole dish with the cover

that's on the floor over there?" I suggested. A casserole dish in a bedroom was *so* out of place. It seemed like a logical choice.

The curator smiled at me. "Very good. What do you suppose they were doing with a casserole dish in a bedroom?"

"It probably wasn't a casserole dish," Lyddy began thoughtfully.

"Right so far."

"It's a chamber pot, isn't it?" Christine said.

"Yes!"

The rest of us looked at each other and shrugged. Mrs. McNulty had this expression on her face as if she'd smelled something bad.

"Well, have any of you seen a bathroom in this house?" the curator asked us.

"Oh, no," Lyddy groaned as she rolled her eyes in anticipation of what was coming.

"They used outhouses back then," the curator explained, "but if you got up in the night—say a cold night in January—would you want to get dressed for a trip outdoors to go to the bathroom? No! You'd use a chamber pot, and you'd be darn glad to have one."

"How do you suppose they used them?" Butch said thoughtfully.

It was something I preferred not to suppose about.

"You mustn't touch it, anyone. It's very valuable,"

the curator pointed out. "For all we know, Jonathan Tarbutt, the Revolutionary War hero, may have used it himself."

"Ooooh. Did you hear that, class?" Mrs. McNulty asked, suddenly more enthusiastic. "Now that's *real* history."

"But, you know, it still isn't all that gross," Spike pointed out.

"All right. I'll try one more time. How did they empty their chamber pots?"

Everyone shrugged.

"They dumped them out the window!" the curator exclaimed merrily.

There was a stunned silence, but only for a moment.

"That's beyond gross to disgusting."

"Is that gross enough for you, Butch?"

"I'm satisfied."

"I can't wait to go home and tell my mother what I learned on my field trip."

The curator laughed gleefully.

When we got back outside, Mrs. McNulty pulled a sheet of paper out of the large purse she'd been carrying all morning. "Our next stop," she announced, "will be the herb garden."

Spike looked at me and winked. "You see, the chamber-pot woman was too cool. So now McNutty has to take us to a boring place to sort of balance things out."

"We have an herb garden at my house," I said coldly.

"And it's boring, isn't it? Isn't it? You don't have to answer. I know I'm right."

He was.

• • •

Our last stop before lunch was a shed that looked as if it had been built recently, but built to look old like the house. There were huge gaps between the boards that had to let in wind and rain, which would have been a huge improvement over the intense sun that poured through them while we sat gasping for breath at our assigned seats on hard, backless benches. While we waited for a frail, elderly woman named Miss Flannery to mutter and flutter over an antique VCR we made fans out of our Tarbutt Homestead brochures and waved them in front of our faces and necks or, in Butch's case, underarms.

"I'd like to talk to the children for a little bit before we start the tape. Would that be all right?" Miss Flannery asked.

"As if we have a choice," Spike muttered to the left of me.

"Be our guest," Butch called cheerily to the right of me.

"Thank you. Who can tell me something they've learned about the life of Jonathan Tarbutt, the Revolutionary War hero?"

Three hands shot up in the air. One was chosen.

"He had a cool last name."

"Do you think so?" Miss Flannery asked very seriously.

"Spike," Mrs. McNulty warned.

"He raised his hand," Butch complained. "Geez."

"What else have you learned about Jonathan Tar . . . butt?" Miss Flannery asked.

"Jonathan Tarbutt was the man who would have been chosen to lead the Continental Army if George Washington hadn't wanted the job," Lyddy announced.

"Exactly," Miss Flannery said. "He *almost led the Continental Army.* What do we know about his character? Yes, dear?"

"He was a patriot," one of the girls from Ms. Napolitano's class answered.

"Oh, yes, Jonathan Tarbutt was a great patriot. What else?"

"He was brave," someone replied.

"Oh, Jonathan Tarbutt was very brave."

"And smart."

"Jonathan Tarbutt was very smart indeed."

Butch's hand shot up. "Did Jonathan Tarbutt swim naked in the brook out back the way his boy cousins did?"

"We do know that he spent part of the summer of 1769 here. I suppose he may have," Miss Flannery answered thoughtfully. "Yes, I think it's reasonable to think he may have gone swimming here."

"Are we going to get a chance to see the brook in

which he swam naked?" Spike asked politely. "It would be very educa—"

"No," Mrs. McNulty broke in. "There will be no tours of the swimming hole."

"Did Jonathan Tarbutt actually live in the house you're visiting this morning?" Miss Flannery continued. She didn't wait for a reply but said, "No, he did not, did he? This was his uncle's house. Does anyone know anything about the house Jonathan Tarbutt actually lived in?"

I raised my hand. "It was torn down at the beginning of this century, and there's a store that rents videotapes there now."

"Dirty videotapes," Spike added.

"Yes, there is an adult video store at the site of Jonathan Tarbutt's home. Isn't that too bad? We're so lucky to have this lovely house here to give us some idea of how he lived. Not every state is fortunate enough to have a historical figure like Jonathan Tarbutt. Why, if Washington hadn't wanted to lead the Continental Army, Jonathan would have done it. And if he had led the Continental Army, our Jonathan Tarbutt might have been the first president of these United States."

"And then our nation's capital would be Tarbutt, D.C.," Spike pointed out. "And Tarbutt's name and face would be on our one-dollar bills."

"Yes," Miss Flannery agreed, her head nodding. "It's something to think about, isn't it?"

Spike raised his hand. "Miss Flannery? My cousin,

Butch's oldest brother, did a research paper on Jonathan Tarbutt when he was a senior in high school. And he learned that Jonathan Tarbutt was a close friend of Benedict Arnold's, the Revolutionary War traitor."

Miss Flannery's small gray head went up and down. "That's another thing we can say about Jonathan. He was a good friend."

"According to my cousin, Jonathan was planning to go over to the British, too, but when Benedict Arnold got caught he chickened out."

"That can't be true," Lyddy sneered. "That would mean Jonathan Tarbutt was a traitor and a coward."

"I forgot about Mac's paper," Butch exclaimed. From the look on his face, I guessed it was beginning to come back to him. "He got an A on it, you know."

"Actually," I said in response to Lyddy, "if Spike's right, wouldn't it be more accurate to say that Jonathan Tarbutt was too much of a coward to be a traitor?"

"Oh, come on," Donny laughed. "A Couture got an A on a paper?"

"Mrs. McNulty!" Lyddy complained. "Should they be talking like this?"

"This discussion comes under the category of Rude Talk, and it *will* be punished!" Mrs. McNulty announced.

"There was a great deal of gossip about Jonathan," Miss Flannery said wisely. "That's still another thing we can say about him.

"And now," she continued as she carefully ignored

Butch, who clearly had plenty more to say about his brother's term paper, "it's time for our videotape."

• • •

At lunchtime we spread across the Homestead lawn. It was the absolutely hottest part of the day and we were turned out into it, exposed and unprotected and in alphabetical order.

"You look awful," Butch told me.

"Fair-haired people have to be careful out in the sun," I sighed as I carefully folded up my empty lunch bag.

Butch stretched out on the ground, rolled onto his stomach, and groaned. "The ozone layer is thinning, you know."

"*I* know. I didn't know *you* did."

"What do you think Butch is? Stupid? Just because he gets terrible grades? Ha! And you call yourself a Teddy Scholar!" Spike laughed.

"I didn't learn about this ozone business at school. They don't teach you cool stuff like that there. You have to read *Newsweek* and the newspaper to learn about how the thinning ozone layer is going to cause climatic changes, crop failures, mutations." Butch paused and smiled. "It's going to be like living in a comic book or on a weird planet. I can't wait!"

"Well," Spike sighed, "in the meantime, we're stuck in this heat."

Donny came over to say, "We're leaving in half an

hour. If you want anything from the museum shop, now's the time to get it."

"Half an hour, huh? We might be able to do it in that much time," Spike said as he scrambled to his feet.

"Well, my mother gave me money for the museum store, so I guess I'd better go buy a Tarbutt Homestead refrigerator magnet or key chain or something." I could feel sweat bubbling out of my pores. I tried not to think about tussy-mussies.

Spike waved his hand and shouted, "We'll be right along, Mrs. McNulty." Then he turned to his cousin and said, "And we will, too—in about a half an hour."

"What's the plan?" Butch asked.

"To look for Jonathan Tarbutt, the Revolutionary War hero's, swimming hole."

Butch beamed. "Neat."

"Mrs. McNulty said no," I reminded them.

"Mrs. McNulty said, 'No tours.' We're going to go for a swim," Spike explained.

"Why?" I asked. "You know you'll get in trouble."

Butch shook his head. "Somebody has to catch us first."

"Which isn't going to happen, right?" Spike said, looking at me.

What was I supposed to say? "Nah, nah, nah-nah, nah, nah, I'm going to tell"? I had to sit next to those two, which was no treat even when they *weren't* mad at me.

I stood up. Nobody looks tough sitting on the ground with their lunch bag on their lap. "I'm not covering for you," I told Spike.

"You don't have to. Just don't do anything."

"You could come with us," Butch offered.

Leave a field trip to go swimming? I'd never even considered doing anything like that in my whole life. I'd never had a chance.

"No," I said. "I can't."

I watched them walk off together, trying to look casual, and thought of the cold water they were going to be sinking into. Maybe I could go wading with them, I thought as I tried to pick my wet shirt off my chest. Wading wouldn't be wrong, would it? I took a few steps, starting to follow them.

"What did you ask him for?" I heard Spike complain.

"If he was with us, he couldn't snitch," Butch replied as they went around the corner of the old house.

I'll take a shower when I get home, I promised myself. A cold one. A shower would be better than a swim in some filthy brook, anyway. Bacteria. That was what you found in swimming holes.

• • •

"These are switches," I heard Mrs. McNulty explaining to a small group of girls from our class when I finally reached the gift shop. "In the good old days, teachers were allowed to use them on students who misbehaved."

"They hit kids?" Christine asked. It was one of those

informational questions. You could tell she knew the answer. She just wanted to be certain all the other listeners got the point.

"Oh, sure. All the time. And the kids liked it. They appreciated being taught how to behave properly. Nowadays the best we can do for children is put them in alphabetical order," Mrs. McNulty sighed. "It's not much."

Then she paused and looked around the shop. "Where's Butch?" Her gaze fell on what I was afraid was my very guilty face. "Jasper, dear, have you seen Butch and Spike?"

"I saw them a few minutes ago," I squeaked.

"Where were they?"

"Ah . . . on the lawn. We had lunch together."

Mrs. McNulty sighed. "I'd better go look for them."

They're in for it now, I thought. And if they think I snitched, so am I.

"Do you want me to go look for them, Mrs. McNulty?" I offered.

What was wrong with the woman? I wondered. Couldn't she tell there was something wrong just by listening to me? But she just tapped my shoulder with the switch she was still holding and said, "Thank you, dear. You're a wonderful help," while Lyddy rolled her eyes and Christine gave me a suspicious look.

I ran toward the meadow in back of the house. I found the brook at its far end, right where the forest began. When I got there I could hear the sound of splashing and laughing. I ran along the brook until I found a spot in the trees where it was wider and deeper than at other places. And there I also found Butch and Spike in water up to their necks and looking cooler than I'd felt since May.

"Come on, you guys!" I shouted. "Mrs. McNulty's looking for you!"

"What is wrong with that woman?" Spike howled. "She has really ruined this field trip for me."

"I don't think I learned a thing," Butch said just before he threw himself forward into the dead man's float.

I think several more things were said about how awful the field trip had been, but I didn't actually hear them. What I did hear was myself gasping.

"You're . . . naked!" I finally managed to wheeze as Butch's white bottom bobbed along on the top of the water.

"Well, sure. How did you think we'd go swimming? In our sneakers?" Spike asked from where he was squatting and splashing.

"Yup, we decided to swim just like ol' Jonathan Tar-butt, the Revolutionary War hero." Butch laughed as he lifted his wet head out of the water and shook it.

"Where are your clothes?" I sputtered. "How are you going to dry yourselves? Did you bring towels?"

"Towels?" Spike repeated. "What kind of idiot brings towels on a field trip? We're going to air-dry."

"Then you'd better get started," a voice said be-hind me.

I was the only guy there with clothes on. I was also the only guy there who seemed at all concerned that Mrs. McNulty had joined us.

"They . . . went for a swim in the brook," I whispered without turning around.

"And they're going to get out of it *right now.*"

The Cootches looked at each other, and then Spike smiled at Mrs. McNulty.

"Never let it be said that a Cootch didn't do what he was told," he said as they both stood up.

Four

I Didn't Get It

It's been five years or more since even my mother has seen me naked. I had to admit it must have taken guts—or something—for the Cootches to walk out of that brook and march by Mrs. McNulty with those great big grins on their faces.

They weren't grinning when they returned to class after their four-day, in-school suspension, though.

"I was trying to help you!" I insisted when they caught me outside Mrs. McNulty's room.

"Help us? You led her right to us!" Spike yelled.

We were out by our lockers. I had never actually believed those stories about kids being shoved into one of those things, but they were weighing heavily on my mind as I stood with my back against mine.

"How could I have known she was going to see me out in the meadow and follow me?"

"How could you not?" Butch asked. "It's only in every movie and television show ever made. The person who tries to contact the people in hiding are *always* followed by the bad guy."

"Jasper only watches The Learning Channel, Butch," Spike said in disgust. "That's why he doesn't know anything."

"What was I supposed to do when she said she was going to look for you?" I asked.

"Nothing! You were supposed to do nothing!" Spike said without even thinking about it. "She would never have found us. All you had to do was keep your mouth shut and *do nothing.*"

I figured there was no winning an argument with the Cootches, so I just threw my hands up.

"Still want to ask them to get together for a group meeting on the West Adams project?" Lyddy asked as we watched them wander into our classroom.

"We have to do something. There's only two and a half weeks left until it's due, and we haven't even planned it."

Lyddy and I had checked in with Mrs. McNulty earlier, so we headed toward our Teddy Scholars meeting on Birds of the Arctic.

"I think we should just do it ourselves," Lyddy said.

"We can't. It's a group project," I objected.

"That's fine if you have a decent group. But ours isn't even average. I understand Mrs. McNulty placing us with Butch and Spike—we are the best students in the class, so we'll balance them. But why dump Donny and

Christine on us, too? Donny would have been my first choice—*if* we were playing baseball. But as far as school's concerned he can't even organize his binder correctly. And Christine? You've noticed, of course, that Señora Wahlburg avoids calling on her in Spanish class. If you sat in the flute section of the band, the way I do, you'd know that sometimes she just pretends to be playing . . . which is a very good idea when you consider how badly she reads music. I've never seen her report card, of course, but I bet the marking periods when she doesn't have at least one C are few and far between. She's not good at anything.

"We should feel sorry for them, I know, but group projects are averaged and those two and the Cootches are going to pull ours down. Remember, Jasper, this is an important year for us. The Theodore Ervin Memorial Award for EVERYTHING should be ours."

"And Kimberly Stafford's," I reminded her.

"She's getting *nothing* if I have anything to say about it. What we need to do is divide up the work, so . . ."

"That's why we need to have a meeting," I suggested.

"No. I mean you and I should divide up the work. We'll just forget about the others."

But we didn't.

We had two meetings (sort of) during the free periods we got each week and accomplished an amazingly small amount of work during each of them. I offered to have a third one the next Saturday morning. I called both Butch and Spike at home Friday night to remind them. Butch said he might come if I could guarantee we'd have food. Spike refused even to speak to me. I had to leave a message with his mother.

"You're crazy to let the Cootches in your house," Lyddy told me soon after she and Donny arrived. "I wouldn't even let them know where I live."

"Well, they were so noisy during the meetings at school," I reminded her.

"You think they won't be noisy here?"

"They'll be guests in my parents' home. They ought to be on their best behavior," I said hopefully.

Donny laughed. "Butch and Spike on their best behavior. I can't wait."

"You could have saved yourself a lot of trouble—and me, too—if we'd just done this project ourselves. It would have been a whole lot easier, and we'd have been sure of an A," Lyddy complained.

"We'd be lying if we said they did it when they didn't. It's a group project. We're supposed to do it as a group."

"Just a minute here," Donny said. "If you and Lyddy did the project by yourselves, would we all get an A?"

"Let me explain how a group project works," Lyddy began.

Donny had heard enough. "Well, gee, Jasper, if I can get an A for sure if you do it . . ."

"Let *me* explain how a group project works!" I said. "Doesn't anyone understand the meaning of the word *group*?"

Mom came into the dining room where we were waiting for the others. "Don't anyone panic, but there are two very rough-looking kids roaming around our yard."

"That's got to be Butch and Spike!" Donny exclaimed as we all ran to the front door.

Sure enough, there they were right in the middle of my father's perennial garden. Dad was squatting down in front of them, explaining, I'm sure, that Sweet William attracts butterflies, that hosta is a good shade plant, that the moles keep eating his Russell lupine. Butch had his hands clasped behind his back and was nodding his head, doing a fine imitation, in fact, of someone who was awake and listening. Spike, on the other hand, was looking longingly over his shoulder, up at the trees, across the lawn to the driveway—any place that was some other place.

It was a common reaction to Dad's perennial tour.

I would have liked to have seen them get a lecture on our vegetable borders, fruit trees, and flowering shrubs as well, but Lyddy began to worry about the dance class she had at eleven o'clock, so we had to call the Cootches in.

"You have a really neat yard, Mr. Gordon," Spike said as he entered the house with my father. "It would be a great place to hide stuff, have battles, bury things."

"Oh, no, no, boys. These are ornamental gardens. They're only for looking at, not playing in. Well, it was a pleasure showing you around. It's nice to meet young men with an interest in gardening. A lot of young people really don't care about plants at all," Dad said as he and my mother left us in the living room.

"Would he like to know why?" Butch whispered as he limped (he'd flipped his bicycle on the trip over from Spike's house) into the dining room. His head dropped onto his chest and he started to snore.

"What is this supposed to be?" Spike asked as he picked a cheese Danish up off the platter my mother had put out for us.

"Food," Donny explained as he helped himself to another.

There was also sour cream coffee cake and croissants.

"I thought there'd be jelly doughnuts," Butch complained. He took the lid off the juice pitcher. "Is there Pepsi in here?"

Spike laughed. "The Burpmeister *loves* Pepsi."

Lyddy cringed and then looked at me. "We're doing a project with someone who calls himself the Burpmeister! And it's all your fault!"

Spike turned on me, too. "That's true. If you hadn't told my mother about this project last night, Butch and I would never have had to show up here today. Never, ever. You are never to talk to my mother again. Never, ever."

"Oh, yeah, you really got Aunt Evie going. Now that she knows there's a social studies project due we're actually going to have to do it. My father has started kicking my backside about my grades just because he can't stand listening to Aunt Evie complain about Spike and me anymore. Nobody can reason with her."

"She's been out of her mind since second grade, when I got straight A's all year," Spike explained. He sounded disgusted.

"All year?" Lyddy and I repeated together.

Spike nodded. "What a disaster that was. But who would have known that bringing my mother a few perfect report cards would mean she'd be on me the rest of my life?"

Donny grinned. "I've never brought my mother perfect report cards, and she's still been on me all my life."

I sighed. We had two tests the next week I needed to study for that weekend. I had to make school Open House posters for the special advertising project we were doing in Teddy Scholars. There was science and math homework for Monday, I had a Boy Scout meeting in a few hours, Sunday School the next morning, two saxophone practices before I went to bed Sunday night, and my aunt and cousins were coming for dinner sometime very soon.

"Can we get this show on the road?" I asked.

"As soon as Chrissie gets here," Butch replied. He was eating from a serving plate, which he was holding on his lap so no one else could get to it.

"She's not coming," I announced.

"Oh? And how come she doesn't have to come?"

"It's not as if she'd have done much."

"Does she get to share our grade if she doesn't do anything?"

"Not everybody's here—we should just forget the whole thing."

"Christine's mother was called in to work unexpectedly this morning, and Christine has to take care of her younger brother and sisters. I'll call her after the meeting and tell her what we decide," I told them.

"We're going to decide that Lyddy is not going to be group leader," Spike announced, picking up on an argument that had continued through both our first meetings. "No one would follow her out of a burning building."

"I think Spike or I should be leader. It's a project on the town of West Adams, right? Well, our family has lived in West Adams for hundreds of years. In fact, our beloved ancestor, Etienne Couture, was one of the founding fathers of the town," Butch bragged.

"We should have known a Couture was responsible for this pit," Lyddy said. "I think that's a very good reason why neither one of you should be leader."

"Maybe we can get along without a leader," I suggested.

"Impossible. Groups have to have leaders," Lyddy insisted.

"You're not going to be leader," Spike sang.

"Would everybody be happy if Donny or Christine were the leader?" I asked.

"Oh, I don't want to be leader."

"Oh, come on, Donny! You can just pretend to be leader," I pleaded.

"Well, if he's just pretending, we might as well not have a leader at all," Lyddy pouted.

"That what I said," I reminded her. "Why don't you each just research and write your own papers on one organization or event in town. I'll put all the general facts about the town into an introduction and then make sure all the parts fit together as one report."

Spike shook his head. "Nope. That makes you leader."

"*You* can put it together and write the introduction then. It doesn't matter."

"Not very likely."

"We'd only have to write about one thing?" Donny asked.

I nodded my head.

"Gee, Jasper, that sounds awfully good."

"It sounds as if you'll be the leader," Spike grumbled.

"I won't be the leader!" I shouted. "I'll just be doing the extra work!"

"That works for me," Butch said happily.

It worked for everybody.

• • •

Time passed, and still it seemed to me that *some* people weren't doing a whole lot.

"It's due next Friday. I've got to have it soon!" I insisted one day when we were waiting in line to come in from recess.

"Keep your pants on," Spike told me.

"I'm not the one who has trouble keeping my pants on," I reminded him. "But I'm going to have trouble organizing this paper if I don't get your sections soon. Lyddy's been done for a week and a half. Even Donny and Christine have given me their sections."

" 'Even' Donny and Christine?" Donny repeated. "What's that supposed to mean?"

"Uh . . ."

"Remind me—why do we have to turn all our work in to you before it goes to Mrs. McNutty? What's so special about you?" Spike wanted to know.

"Oh, no. Don't start this again," Lyddy begged.

"I'm going to type everything up so it looks the same. I'm going to fix everything!"

"My stuff doesn't need fixing," Spike bragged. "Ms. Spendolini looked at it when Butch and I were in the office during recess last week. She liked it."

"Ms. Spendolini visited you in the Detention Room!" Donny said enviously.

"We became rather friendly while I was serving my suspension."

"And she liked your part of the West Adams project?" I asked in disbelief.

"Then you should be ready to turn it in, shouldn't you?" Lyddy snapped. She had run out of patience with this assignment about five days earlier.

"You'll have it in plenty of time," Spike said.

"I don't want to change it," I promised. "I'll just do a little editing."

"He *is* coeditor of the literary magazine, after all. He *knows* what he's doing."

I thought I could have done without Lyddy's help in that particular battle.

"Ah! The literary magazine! I have this idea we can use in the literary magazine . . ."

"We?" Lyddy repeated.

"Please, Spike. Can't we stick to the town of West Adams project—which is due a week from today?" I begged.

"Ms. Spendolini thought this was a very interesting idea," Spike continued.

"Yeah, she did," Butch agreed. "I heard her."

"Ms. Spendolini liked it?" I said uncertainly. I didn't get it. Ms. Spendolini hardly knew I was alive, but she thought someone who lost his recess on a weekly basis and had served a suspension for getting naked on a field trip had interesting ideas.

"She said it was very interesting, and it was very clever of me to think of it," Spike said.

"I don't remember her saying you were 'very clever,' " Butch objected.

"Maybe you imagined that part," Lyddy suggested. "Maybe you imagined the whole thing."

"Are you old enough to read *Seventeen?* " Spike asked her nastily.

"Of course, I am. I love *Seventeen*. I read it all the time."

"Even though you're only twelve?" Butch asked.

Christine broke in to the conversation and moved it along by saying that she had read *Seventeen* a few times.

"You ever see that column girls write in to about embarrassing things that have happened to them?" Spike asked her.

"Sure. It's called 'Trauma-rama.' "

"Well, my sister has been getting *Seventeen* for years, and I can tell you that column is the best thing in the whole magazine," Spike declared.

"That's right," Butch added. "The rest of the magazine is about girl problems. But this column? It is *full* of stuff about girls losing the tops of their bathing suits while they're at the ocean and ripping out huge belches in church."

"So," Spike explained, "I was thinking we could do something in the literary magazine that would be like that but different. We could call our column 'Gross Me Out,' and kids could write us letters about raunchy things that have happened to them and we'd print them."

"Forget it!" Lyddy exclaimed.

"Are you sure Ms. Spendolini liked that idea?" Donny asked.

"I never actually said she *liked* it. She thought it was interesting."

"I want your part of the town of West Adams project

on Monday morning!" I ordered. "And I'll be calling your mother Sunday night, Spike, to make sure you bring it in."

He brought it in.

. . .

Mrs. McNulty returned our project to me the Monday after I turned it in. Spike snatched it away from me and read the first sentence of the "General Introduction" out loud.

" 'West Adams is located very near the center of our state with a latitude of 41.40 and a longitude of 73.10.' The whole thing isn't like this, is it?" he asked. "People have died from reading stuff only half as boring as this."

"What you think of it doesn't matter," Lyddy said as she grabbed it out of his hand. "You don't give grades."

The six of us huddled around my table and went over Mrs. McNulty's comments.

General Overview/Introduction
By Jasper Gordon

This is exactly what I was looking for, Jasper. Good use of details. Good introduction to the rest of the paper.

Butch made a particularly slurpy kissing noise near my ear as I turned the page.

The Theodore Ervin Memorial
Elementary School
by Lydia Daniels

Good use of details. Excellent charts. Interesting argument relating to finding more funding for the Teddy Scholars program.

"Hmmm," Spike said. " 'Interesting argument' . . . But did she actually like it? Was it exactly what she was looking for?"

Butch got so excited while reading the next section that he drowned out Lyddy telling Spike to shut up.

The Theodore Ervin
Memorial Volunteer Fire Department
by Butch Couture

Not enough details. For instance, how many people are volunteer firefighters? How many fires do they fight each year? Your pictures and charts are nice enough, but they have little to do with the report. Please say "vomit" instead of "throw up."

"Hey!" Donny laughed. "Butch said 'throw up' in a social studies report!"

"Let's see his pictures," Christine asked, and I flipped to an appendix that contained the diagrams Butch had drawn of the cardiovascular system, cardiopulmonary resuscitation, head and neck trauma, and orthopedic injuries and their treatment to go along with the part of his report describing the fire department's emergency medical services.

"These are beautiful," Christine said.

"You can have 'em," Butch offered.

Christine took another look at a picture of a human heart and said, "Gee. Thanks."

Theodore Ervin, the Man
by Donald Hall

Too short. Omit the last paragraph. Whenever you are writing about people who actually lived you should say only nice things about them.

"Oh, no!" Lyddy moaned. "What did you say about him?"

Donny shrugged. "He left money in his will for four tennis courts and only one baseball diamond. Well," he continued defensively, "a lot more people play baseball than tennis. We need another diamond."

Lyddy sighed and turned her attention to the next section.

The Theodore Ervin Public Library
by Christine Janicki

Where are your details? How many books does the library own? How many of them are fiction? How many are nonfiction? How many hours a week is the library open? There is so much good information about a library. The story you made up about the founder of the library was inappropriate.

"I warned you," Lyddy said to me under her breath. Then she saw what was coming next and said, "We're doomed."

The Coutures of West Adams: A Ballad
by Spike Couture

"The Coutures of West Adams" was a thirty-one-stanza poem (not one word of which I personally believed) about a half dozen of Spike's ancestors, all of whom seemed to have been named Stephen—except for the one who was named Willard. As I had typed it, I hoped we would get credit for length. It covered seven pages, and I had carefully spell-checked the whole thing. That should count for something, I told myself again as I rushed past page after page of rhymed tales of Coutures who had traveled with Lafayette, married Indian princesses, become cowboys, and suffered from motion sickness.

Wrong! Wrong! Wrong!

Spike shook his head. "Maybe she didn't understand it."

"Maybe it STUNK!" Lyddy hissed, her eyes popping with rage.

"Calm down, everybody. We haven't seen a letter grade yet," I said as I turned one more page.

Work is uneven. Paper isn't uniform. Overall grade: B—

"B minus!" Butch exclaimed. "Not too shabby."

"My mother will cry for joy when she hears about this." Spike laughed.

Christine clapped her hands and jumped up and down. Even Donny seemed pleased, though he did remind me that we could have had an A without him having to do anything at all if I had only agreed to do the project with Lyddy.

Lyddy. Her eyes were pink and wet with tears.

"A B minus? A B minus?" she kept repeating, as if she'd never heard of such a thing.

As for me, I'd heard of B minuses but I'd never seen one.

Not up close and personal like that.

Five

It Could Become
Habit Forming . . .
Maybe Not

Lyddy was upset for days about the town of West Adams project and spent a lot of time talking about what we (by which she meant I) could have done differently. It was a great relief when the end of October came and she found something else to complain about.

It began when I saw her approach Mrs. McNulty one morning before class started.

"Mrs. McNulty?" she said respectfully.

"Yes," Mrs. McNulty responded without looking up from her work.

"Halloween is a week from this Friday, and some of us were wondering if we could have a little Halloween party."

Later Lyddy said she had expected Mrs. McNulty to say something like, "Why, of course, dear, what a wonderful idea! We'll do it at one-thirty and have cupcakes and cider." She wasn't at all prepared for Mrs. McNulty to say nothing, so she kept talking—which is, I've learned, almost always a bad move.

"Ah . . . we don't have to wear costumes or anything," Lyddy said. "We could just have some Halloween candy, and maybe we could do something. Maybe you could read us a Halloween story? Christine has one she thinks everyone will like."

Mrs. McNulty threw her pen down and looked up at Lyddy. "Grow up!" she snapped. Then she said she was going to get a cup of coffee and left the room.

"Whoa! Did you see old McNutty blow off Lyddy?" Butch crowed. He and Spike were bent over a couple of brown paper bags they had cut open, stretched out on Spike's and *my* table, and taped together.

"I, for one, am very surprised—shocked, in fact—that the McNutt doesn't want to spend *all day* Friday party-ing. I would have thought Halloween would be the old witch's favorite holiday," Spike replied.

"Maybe she was just trying to tell you we're not kids anymore," I suggested to Lyddy after she crept back to her table.

"She could have said it in a nicer way," Christine said.

"Miss Wilbur is letting her class have a party," Lyddy whimpered. "And Kimberly Stafford says Ms. Napoli-tano always brings her class popcorn balls and those lit-tle orange pumpkin candies on Halloween."

"I didn't like those pumpkin candies when I was a kid," Donny recalled. "I hated getting them for treats."

We all agreed that pumpkin candies were objectionable as trick-or-treat booty but that we wouldn't turn our noses up if a teacher offered them as a gift.

"I used to love to . . . color pumpkins," Christine confided.

"Orange crayons are great," Butch agreed. "And when you're coloring, pumpkin stems are the most perfect green there is. Grass and leaves don't come close."

Lyddy shook her head sadly. "I haven't colored a pumpkin . . . or anything else . . . in years."

"It's better to make pumpkins out of construction paper," I objected. "You can make everything more regular and perfect that way."

"You remember how excited we used to get when the teacher gave us a new sheet of orange construction paper because we thought we were going to make the perfect jack-o'-lantern out of it?" Donny recalled fondly. "We were little kids and we were too stupid to know we couldn't do it or we couldn't remember how awful our last jack-o'-lantern turned out."

"You get excited over construction paper, Hall?" Spike hooted. "Get a life."

"Anybody can make a construction-paper jack-o'-lantern," Butch said. "They're easy to draw, too. Look."

And he leaned over the paper bag he had been working on and quickly dashed off three small jack-o'-lanterns.

"Those are good."

"What are you doing?"

"What is this thing?"

"It's Jasper's front yard," Spike explained. "We're going to haunt it Halloween night."

Jasper who?

I looked down at what was clearly a pencil drawing of the front of my house—complete with headstones, mummies, skeletons, figures hanging from trees, mist, and now, jack-o'-lanterns.

"His front yard is perfect. His father showed us the whole thing that day we were there," Butch pointed out. "And it's in a really nice neighborhood. You can just tell that there'll be lots of little kids out there Halloween night."

Well, sure, but . . .

Spike tapped the mist with one finger. "You have a humidifier, don't you, Jasper? And maybe a few extension cords?"

"I . . . we . . ."

"This looks terrific," Donny said appreciatively.

"It's going to be very, very cool," Spike informed him and anyone else nearby.

"I don't . . . you know . . . and my parents . . ."

"Your father is going to love what we do to his yard," Butch assured me.

Ah, my father, I thought with a smile. My father, who always lined our path with milk bottles filled with sand and candles to discourage trick-or-treaters from walking on his grass. . . . My father, who always raked the lawn the day after Halloween to make sure nothing had been dropped there that might get caught in his lawnmower. . . . My father, who once suggested that we park the car next to the road and hand our treats out from the trunk because he just seeded six weeks before. . . .

My father would put an end to this, I thought confidently.

• • •

On Saturday Dad looked down at the Cootches' plan and rubbed his chin thoughtfully.

"Well, Spike, you're certainly right that the skeletons hanging from the flowering dogwoods will draw attention to their fall foliage. But what about these plastic heads of yours—you say you put Glow Sticks in them? How about if you line our walk with them?" he suggested.

"What a great idea, Mr. Gordon," Butch exclaimed. "We could call it 'The Avenue of Death.' And anybody who wants candy will have to pass through it!"

Dad said he liked the sound of that, too.

"Oh, boy!" Mom squealed. "Can I have a costume?"

And that explains how I came to be stuffing a pair of Spike's sister's pants with newspaper the following Wednesday after school.

"This has been an awful lot of work," I pointed out, thinking of the toilet-paper pharaoh's mummy, the milk-bottle skeletons, and the various headstones we'd made since Sunday afternoon, to say nothing of this figure we'd been working on since Butch's father had let the Cootches off in front of my house that day.

"You don't know what hard work is," Spike replied as Butch placed a rubber mask over the newspaper sticking out of the neck of Pam Couture's sweatshirt. "One year we built a false front for our porch and made a real haunted house behind it. Now *that* was hard work."

"So why aren't you doing something at your own house this year?" I asked.

"Oh, well, you know how parents are . . ." Spike said vaguely.

My father had just spent twenty-five dollars on Glow Sticks for the Cootches' plastic heads, and my mother was making herself a Princess Leia costume. I didn't know anything about how *my* parents were, let alone anyone else's.

Butch gave a satisfied sigh and looked down at the lumpy and ugly man lying at our feet. "This is going to be scary," he said happily.

"I don't get what's so spooky about hobos," I objected.

"Granny Couture was very scared of hobos when she was a girl," Butch explained. "She's always telling us about them."

"Are we expecting Granny Couture here Halloween?" I asked.

"*This* particular hobo is going to be scary because he's going to be sitting in a lawn chair holding an ax covered with blood. Let's try to prop him up in a chair now. Then we can hide him here in your garage until Halloween."

He began to go over his Halloween plans. "We have all the major figures made. Are you going to have an extension cord for us, Jasper? And we're each going to bring a jack-o'-lantern. You promise your jack-o'-lantern will be ugly, Jasper? You won't carve it so it looks like a kitten or anything? Good. I think we'd better wash the plastic heads the next time we're here."

"The next time you're here?"

"We'll come by tomorrow and finish up."

"I don't think we can get together tomorrow."

"We have to. Halloween is the next day," Spike said.

"We've spent so much time on this Halloween stuff that I haven't been able to spend as much time on my homework as I should. So I want . . . to do . . . some of that . . . tomorrow," I finished.

There was a long pause.

"You are out of your mind, you know," Spike said at last.

"You can do homework anytime!" Butch howled. "This is Halloween we're talking about."

"I've never had to do this much for Halloween before," I objected.

"You couldn't have had much fun, then," Butch replied.

That was true. Still . . .

"I usually do my homework right after school," I said. "I'm in soccer this fall, so I have to go to practices a couple of times a week—"

"I play sports," Butch broke in. "It doesn't take up that much time."

"Butch! You've never played a full season of anything in your entire life! You're always getting hurt! Besides, I have Boy Scout stuff to do. And then there's band practice."

Spike shook his head sadly. "You need to set some priorities."

"I have. That's what I'm telling you—"

"I bet you don't have your costume ready, do you?" Spike said.

"I need a costume?"

"I knew it! Of course you need a costume. You can't be yourself. You do two drafts on book reports—"

"Sometimes three," I broke in.

"Nobody's going to be afraid of you, Jasper," Butch said, finishing Spike's thought.

"Nobody has to be afraid of me. *You're* going to be here."

We were still fighting about whether or not I was going to dress up when Spike's sister arrived to take them home, saw her clothes on our hobo, and began a second fight right there in my garage.

"Thanks for coming," I called when they finally roared out of my driveway.

• • •

When Butch and Spike arrived at our house on Halloween, we were still eating dinner.

"You're not done yet?" Butch asked in amazement as Dad led him and Spike into the dining room.

We never actually answered that question (wasn't it obvious?) because we were distracted by the sound of tires squealing out in front of the house.

"Who was that?" Mom exclaimed.

"My brother, Doug," Butch assured her. "He dropped us off."

"And what's he doing for Halloween?" Dad asked.

Butch shrugged. "You'll read about it in the paper tomorrow."

Mom laughed merrily. "I love that boy's sense of humor," she said to Dad.

"Hurry up, Jasper," Butch ordered. "We've got lots to do before people start arriving."

"Why don't you boys get started while Jasper finishes his dinner, clears his place, loads the dishwasher, and brushes his teeth," Dad suggested.

"That's a good idea," Spike replied in a tone of voice that said very plainly that he didn't think it was a good idea at all.

By the time I was through Butch and Spike had positioned the hobo in his lawn chair by the front door and the pharaoh in its coffin out by the fence. They were carefully lining their plastic head collection along each side of our path.

"What do you think?" Spike wanted to know. "Should they look as if they're talking to each other or should they all be pointed as if they're staring at the little kids as they walk up to the front door?"

"I think," Butch said, sounding very thoughtful, "they should stare at the little kids. We want it to look as if the heads have been *waiting* for all the lovely little boys and girls."

Oh, yes, all the lovely little boys and girls were going to love that, I thought.

After much fiddling with extension cords we got my humidifier spewing a nice mist behind the cardboard headstones. I supposed anybody who'd ever had a really bad case of bronchitis would find it terrifying.

"I bet you've never seen your yard look so good, huh?" Spike inquired.

It *was* an improvement on my father's brown and orange mums.

"It's getting dark. We'd better get into our costumes."

Butch rubbed his hands together happily as he ran over to the steps and picked up a paper bag.

I offered, with some reservations, my own bedroom to the Cootches to use as a changing room. After watching them safely up the stairs I darted out the front door to get into my costume.

When Butch and Spike reappeared they found Mom in her old white bathrobe with brown yarn balls pinned to the sides of her head and a dime-store plastic space weapon in her hand. "Let the force be with you!" she shouted as the three of them posed for my father. I was waiting out front and could hear and see all of them through the open front door.

"I'm not sure I know who you're supposed to be," Mom said after she'd had her picture taken shooting at each of them.

Their costumes *were* a little on the simple side. They both wore old (and too large) blazers and dress shirts with scarves knotted around their necks, and they both carried fat wooden dowels with old glass doorknobs jammed on the end of them.

"We're Dr. Jekyll and Mr. Hyde," Spike explained as if Mom should have known better than to ask.

"Yeah. A hundred years ago all the coolest guys dressed like this," Butch told her. "And, believe it or not, these costumes didn't cost us a cent."

"Which one of you is which?" Dad asked.

All he got for a response was a long, low rumble

that had to have come from somewhere deep in Butch's gut.

"Oh. I see," Dad said.

I would never have done that in front of Butch's father. For that matter, I would've never done it in front of mine.

"So where's Jasper?" Butch asked. "I hope he didn't dress up in something embarrassing like a gift box or a television set."

"I think he went outside," Mom said absently as she admired her hair in our hall mirror.

Butch and Spike ran out on the steps and looked around.

"I don't see him anywhere. Maybe he's doing something out back," Butch suggested.

I held my breath and watched Spike pace back and forth between the pharaoh and the humidifier. I had to pick the perfect time, I knew, to make this thing work. But what was the perfect time?

"There's nothing to do out back," Spike said as he hesitated near the hobo.

Now? I wondered.

"You know Jasper," Spike went on. "He probably decided it was time to put clean sheets on his bed."

Now! I decided.

"Or," Spike continued, "maybe he just chickened ou . . . YOW!"

Spike jumped, and Butch used a few words that hadn't been heard in our yard since a workman replacing windows put his hand through a pane of glass.

"Is that you, Jasper?" Butch gasped.

"Jasper?" Spike said in disbelief.

The screen door slammed as both my parents ran out onto the front step. They arrived just in time to see me rip the hobo's rubber mask off my head.

"Jasper?" they both said doubtfully.

What a triumph! There I stood, in front of the hobo's chair, wearing his clothes, and holding his stained ax. I could grow to like this, I thought. It could become habit forming. I—

"Damn it, Jasper," Spike roared, his voice full of rage.

Well, maybe not.

Everything stopped, just like they talk about in books. My parents and I stared at Spike as if we thought he was going to blow up. My father's bigger than he is, I thought. And my mother can scream for help. And me? I supposed I could run.

"Damn it, Jasper," Spike repeated. "You scared me so badly I almost wet my pants."

Oh, no! I almost made Spike Couture wet his pants. What had I been thinking of?

"Good job!" Butch cried.

Spike threw his arms around me. "You're going to have the parents screaming and begging for mercy!"

That seems to be a good thing, I thought as I collapsed onto the lawn chair.

"Listen," Butch cried. "I can hear them."

We all turned toward the road. We could just make out lights bobbing along in the darkness.

"Quick! Jasper, get back into the chair!"

"Quick! Spike, you stand at the corner of the house and look scary!"

"Quick! John, get the video camera!"

"Quick! Butch, get ready to run out from behind that tree waving your cane!"

Everyone got into position. I scrunched down into my chair, trying to look as much like a fake hobo as possible. I hugged my ax and smiled until my face hurt under my mask.

This is going to be great, I thought. It's going to be so great.

"So you really almost wet your pants?" I asked Spike.

"Shut up, Jasper."

Six

A Joy to Have
in Class

So what happened?" Donny kept asking me the following week. "And then what?"

"These two little kids started crying, and their mother got mad," I explained once. "They kept coming back, though, because every time they started to wail my father gave them extra candy. We couldn't get rid of them. Spike had a can of that spray cheese and kids kept chasing him around trying to get him to spray it into their mouths. That was kind of messy. And then there were other kids who screamed and spilled their candy out of those plastic pumpkins, which was how Butch got the gum that pulled two brackets off his teeth."

"So you had a good time, huh?"

I shrugged. "I guess. Everybody on the street ended up in our yard. My father had to go out for more candy. But ever since Halloween the neighbors point at me whenever they drive by and see me outside."

Donny laughed. "You must have had a *really* good time."

Evidently, so did the Cootches.

"I think they like you now," Donny said after a couple of weeks. "Oh, yeah. You can tell when they don't like somebody. Twice yesterday Spike could have pounded you with the volleyball in gym class, but he didn't. He's not good at gym, but he can always hit what he's aiming at if it's another kid."

"Butch has started calling me at home," I admitted.

Donny grimaced. "Does he threaten you? Talk dirty?"

I shook my head. "Mostly he wants to talk about what he's watching on television. He calls during commercials."

Donny relaxed and nodded. "Oh, he definitely likes you. What about Spike? Does he call?"

"No, he just rides his bicycle up and down my street all the time. Evidently he lives a whole lot closer to me than I thought." Or liked.

"Does he throw stuff on your lawn? Shout things? No? Then you've got it made. He likes you, too. Promise me that if either one of them invites you to their house you'll bring me with you. I've never had a chance to see where they live."

"I'm sure not going there by myself," I replied.

I sure wouldn't have looked at Spike's first marking period report card, either, if he hadn't kept shoving it in my face over and over again.

"You want to see something? Do you? Take a look at that," Spike kept demanding.

I couldn't help myself. There was a set of letter grades like none I'd ever seen before.

"No, not that. Look at the comments," Spike ordered.

"'Doesn't accept authority well. Is disrespectful toward adults. Does not work up to potential because insists on doing everything own way. Needs to learn self-discipline. Wastes time on subjects that have nothing to do with school. And, of course, there was the field trip.'"

"This is a perfect example of how unreasonable the McNutt is."

I would have added, "Doesn't get along well with others," but perhaps Mrs. McNulty didn't want to overwhelm Mr. and Mrs. Couture with bad news.

"Look! Look! No F's!" Butch exclaimed as he danced around in front of our lockers, waving his report card in Lyddy's face.

"There are two D minuses," she pointed out.

"But no F's. I'm rather proud of the fact that I've never had an F, and I was sure Mrs. McNutty was going to ruin my good record and fail me in something. She doesn't give us any time at the end of classes to start our homework the way our other teachers did, so I'm having trouble keeping up."

Donny said he was, too. "I sometimes have two hours of homework a night this year."

"You do it at home?"

"Of course, we do it at home. That's why it's called homework, Butch. When do you do it?" I asked.

"I don't. School is for schoolwork. If Mrs. McNutty can't arrange her time well enough so I can get my work done at school, then she's just out of luck," Butch explained as he packed his textbooks in his locker.

"And you've never failed *anything?*" Lyddy asked. She looked as if she found that hard to believe.

"Never. In fact, until the end of fourth grade I didn't do badly. When I saw Mrs. McNutty was too disorganized to leave us class time, I thought I was done for. I must be smarter than I thought."

"She's not disorganized. She just covers more material in class than the teachers in the lower grades did," I explained as I loaded my backpack for the trip home. "There's more to do now, Butch."

"You don't have to suck up to her today, Jasper. We had a sub, remember?" Spike said—in the nicest possible way, though.

I gritted my teeth and consoled myself with the brief "A joy to have in class" that appeared on my report card.

Christine leaned weakly against her locker. "I always got an A in reading. Most times it was the only A I got. But it was always there, and I could always say, 'Well, I've had straight A's in reading, anyway.'"

Her voice broke, and Butch took her report card away from her.

" 'B plus,' " he read. "That's good. And you don't have anything below a C."

"I always get C's. But I had an A in reading for years and years. It was my A."

Christine opened her locker and silently buried her face in the hand-me-down jacket that was hanging in it.

"Help her get her stuff together, Butch. She's going to miss the bus," I said as I reached into my backpack for tissues.

"Okay. Here's your jacket, Christine."

"Come on, Butch! We have an adverb test tomorrow. She needs her book. Make sure she has her binder. Did she get her math done? Pack that, too," I ordered.

"I never bring that much stuff home," Spike said in amazement.

"Maybe that explains your report card," I said as I started down the hall.

That's a good way to get the last word with Spike—say something, and then warp out of there.

• • •

Butch came back to school the next day thinking he was a scholar.

"Wait until you hear the cool article I cut out of the paper for current events," he said as he followed me to the tables. "It's about projectile vomiting. Have you ever heard of that?"

"Butch, we don't have current events today. It's only on Thursdays and Fridays," I told him.

"Ah, shoot."

"See, this is what is wrong with school," Spike complained. "Today Butch has a newspaper article to talk about, and he can't talk about it because this is not the day we talk about newspaper articles. And when the day for talking about newspaper articles comes around again? He'll have lost it."

"I will not. I can hold on to something for a couple of days."

"It's the Tuesday before Thanksgiving, Butch. We won't be discussing current events for over a week," Lyddy said.

"Oh." Butch looked at his article for a moment, then balled it up and lobbed it into a trash can at the front of the room. "Mrs. McNulty would have loved it, too. It was very scientific."

"See, this is what is wrong with school," Spike said again. "In order to get good grades, you have to do what the teacher wants to do when *she* wants to do it."

"Oh. Is that how it works?" Donny said glumly as he dropped his binder on his table. "Why didn't somebody tell me?"

"And here's another thing that's wrong—the teacher gets to . . ."

Butch interrupted Spike's sermon to explain that his cousin had been grounded until Christmas. I thought he'd got off pretty easy, considering the best comment on his report card was "Does not work up to potential."

Spike shrugged the whole thing off. "Ah, I was grounded for a month after every report card last year. Being at home all the time isn't bad once you get used to it."

"If I were your mother, I'd want you out of the house as much as possible," Lyddy said, but sort of absently, as if she had other things on her mind. She signaled for me to join her near the window.

"How did you do?" she asked me.

"Well, you know. Pretty well."

"I got a B in social studies. You're the only one I'm telling, so if anyone finds out I'll know you told. Kimberly Stafford is supposed to have had A *pluses* in everything but Spanish and math. She just got A's in those."

"A pluses," I repeated, impressed. I myself had been three subjects short of the perfect A plus report card that was my personal goal.

"And I've heard she's doing some kind of special independent project in Teddy Scholars on Great Mountains of the World. It's going to involve lots and lots of papier-mâché. I don't think it will help her, though. Teachers don't like her because she's so stuck on herself. If we can keep our averages high enough, they'll choose you or me over her for the sixth-grade awards. Especially for Student of the Year. Can you imagine anyone wanting her to get that? But that's *if* we can keep our averages high enough. I know I can beat Kimberly in math and science. She's way too dependent on her calculator, and she never even enters the science fair. You'll win that, of course. You always do."

"I'm thinking about a mold project this year," I told her. I had just got the idea a couple of weeks before, and I was pretty excited. "What I want—"

"That will be perfect. And I'll come in second. I should be able to whip Kim's butt in Spanish with no problem, too. Social studies is going to be tricky, though. She is *so* into visual aids, it's disgusting. Maybe we can think of some kind of special social studies project to do that would involve costumes."

"We're studying Egypt now," I reminded her. "They didn't wear much back then."

"That will make the project easier."

"Five minutes. We're starting in five minutes," Mrs. McNulty warned.

"Think about it," Lyddy said as we headed back to our seats.

What kind of costumes? I wondered as I slipped into my chair.

"You know," Spike was saying to Donny, "the literary magazine should run a 'What's Wrong with School' contest. I'd win, of course. It's all so obvious to me. What's wrong with school is that you don't have to be smart to get good grades. You just have to do what you're told."

"So why don't you?" Donny asked.

"Oh, I used to," Spike explained. "I got straight A's in second grade."

"So you've said," I reminded him.

"I did. You can ask anybody."

"So what happened?"

"Well, one week we read *Ramona* in class. And I liked it. I was only in second grade, remember. So I wanted to read the other *Ramona* books. But the teacher said we couldn't. We had to do something else. Then we studied the Navaho. I liked that, too. So, of course, I wanted to study the Arapaho and the Cheyenne and some of those other tribes you see in old movies. But the teacher said we couldn't. We had to do something else.

"I started to notice that that kind of thing was happening a lot. I was always wanting to do something that the teacher said I couldn't do because I had to do something else. So in third grade I just stopped doing the something else I was told I had to do."

"What happened to your grades?" Donny asked.

"They weren't straight A's anymore." Spike grinned. "They weren't straight B's, either."

"Didn't that bother you?" I asked.

Spike just waved the question away. "I was having the time of my life reading everything Beverly Cleary ever wrote *and* every Indian book in the school library. And when I got to the end of third grade and found out you don't need straight A's (or B's or C's, for that matter) to pass, I thought, Gee, why hasn't anyone else ever thought of this? So now I pretty much do what I want."

"And your parents are okay with this?" Donny asked enviously.

"My father swears I'm a better student than he was when he was my age, and my mother . . . well . . ."

"The year Spike was in second grade was the best year of Aunt Evie's life," Butch said. "She still has all his little math papers stuck on her refrigerator. They've turned yellow and the stars have fallen off."

"She has them up there because she thinks it's good for my self-esteem."

Butch shuddered. "They give me the creeps."

"It's always a mistake," Spike told us, "to let anyone know you have two brains to rub together. It only makes trouble."

Butch leaned across the aisle and gave me a nudge. "You're in the most trouble of almost anyone I know," he laughed.

Seven

I Have Something
for You

To: Gordfam@DigMail.net
From: spike@NOL.net
Date: 12/7/9-, 7:46 P.M.
Re: Hello, Jasper
Got your E-mail adress from your mother. Am trying it
out. Let me know if you got this.

To: Gordfam@DigMail.net
From: spike@NOL.net
Date: 12/8/9-, 7:04 A.M.
Re: JG—Last message
Did you get it?

To: Gordfam@DigMail.net
From: spike@NOL.net
Date: 12/8/9-, 2:15 P.M.
Re: Jasper! You have new E-mail
Do you ever check your E-mail?

To: Gordfam@DigMail.net
From: spike@NOL.net
Date: 12/8/9-, 2:23 P.M.
Re: Your butt
I'm going to kick it tomorrow for not returning your E-mail

．．．

The messages started coming the first weekend in December.

For the most part, I don't think Spike was lying when he said he didn't mind being grounded. I couldn't really picture him at the mall buying presents or in a car looking at Christmas lights anyway. I did, however, waste some time I'd planned to use researching my science fair project trying to imagine a little Spike waiting in line to see Santa. It wasn't a pretty picture.

But I guess he must have found the weekends a little slow, because whenever one of my parents went on-line on a Saturday or Sunday they would bring me a little stack of messages they'd downloaded. Most of them were made up of one question about what I was doing and then a short paragraph or so describing what he'd done that day. "Did you study for the Spanish test today? I watched 2 Star Treks (2! back to back). Sucker!" is a good example.

Butch got hold of my E-mail address, too, and wrote me a couple of times while he was home with a stomach flu. But his messages were even shorter and mostly about what he'd been eating just before he got sick.

I risked my butt and didn't return any Cootch E-mail hoping that, just as stray dogs are supposed to go away if you don't feed them, unwanted electronic mail would stop coming if I didn't answer it. Butch would have stopped posting messages anyway. He likes to see or hear his victims as they are being grossed out, and as soon as he was feeling well enough he was back on the telephone or badgering people in person. Spike, however, would have eventually lost interest when he didn't get any response if it hadn't been for Ms. Spendolini.

Ms. Spendolini. Spike called her one serious babe. Butch said he was in love with her. Donny leaped from his chair those mornings she observed our class, catching every question Mrs. McNulty tossed at him and hurling back answers as if he were playing first base again.

And I was beginning to think she was out to get me.

I was supposed to be in the running for Student of the Year, for crying out loud. I was tutoring three—not one, not two, but *three*—third-grade Spanish students. My reading comprehension test scores were so high there was no place for them on the chart. Shouldn't that have bought me a little attention from the principal of my school? Didn't I deserve a few words, a joke, a smile that was for me and for me alone?

Evidently not.

To top everything off, two weeks before Christmas she met me in the hall after my solo at the Holiday Band Concert and said, "Once the holidays are over you need to get started on the literary magazine. I can't wait to see what you guys do."

She sort of nodded over my shoulder and said "you guys" instead of "you," which meant she must have been including Lyddy in her "I can't wait to see what you guys do." It was, I thought, the best thing she'd ever said to me, and it left me feeling that I couldn't wait, either.

Until, that is, I saw Lyddy coming *toward* me with Kimberly Stafford and the rest of the flute section.

Then who's behind me? I wondered. Who's the "guy" in "guys"?

I looked over my shoulder, and, sure enough, there was Spike bobbing along behind me on his way back to class after the concert.

"Don't worry," he said. "This year's literary magazine is going to be the coolest ever. I have *hundreds* of ideas."

Ignoring me was one thing. Ms. Spendolini couldn't give her attention to everyone. But to keep encouraging Spike to horn in on my magazine like that? And while I was right there in the hall with them? Wasn't that just a little mean-spirited?

It certainly got Spike going. Between E-mailing me dozens (not hundreds) of totally unusable ideas for stories, comic strips, surveys, and jokes and constantly calling me to shout, "Go on-line!" he kept the telephone lines between our houses burning for the next two evenings.

When he didn't get any response from me he started showing up at my door.

The first time he was just there, on the step, when I answered the door a couple of days after Christmas. He could have been beamed there for all I knew. I didn't see him arrive or leave.

"Here," he said. "Look at this idea I wrote up for the literary magazine."

"Okay," I said, taking the paper and closing the door.

"Things to Do When Your Board on the Playground" was what he had called it. I didn't have to read it too carefully to know my parents would be on the phone to the school psychologist within five minutes of finding it in my possession. I took a pair of scissors and cut it into the smallest pieces I could manage. Then over the next few hours I flushed it down the toilet.

The next time he came, I had a little warning. I saw him coming between the snowbanks that bordered our driveway on his bicycle. All he had been wearing for a coat since the middle of November was a thin army surplus jacket, so he didn't look as goofy in his winter clothes and bicycle helmet as, say, someone who dressed normally would.

"The last one was just a joke," he began. "This one's for real, and I think you'll like it. Read it right now, and tell me what you think."

"'Top Ten Worst Science Fair Projects,'" I read out loud. I looked at Spike and nodded. This one actually sounded promising.

10. Volcanoes

9. Volcanoes

8. Volcanoes

7. Volcanoes

6. Volcanoes

5. Volcanoes

4. Volcanoes

3. Volcanoes

2. Mold in Little Cups

1. Volcanoes

"Very funny," I said, shoving the paper back at him. *"My* science fair project is on mold."

"You're kidding! Who would have guessed?"

He was laughing all by himself out in the front yard long after I'd closed the door.

And the last time he came, he was with Butch. They were in my living room before I knew they were there.

"Look who's here!" Mom exclaimed happily, after she let them in. "I wish you'd come a little earlier, boys. You could have had lunch with us."

I closed my eyes and breathed a sigh of relief. This, I thought, is why I go to church.

"I have something for you to look at," Spike explained as he held up some colored newsprint.

Butch had his coat off, and Spike was stepping out of his wet sneakers as he spoke. It looked as if they were going to stay a while.

"Oh, go on up to Jasper's room," Mom said. "I'll bring you some ice cream later."

"Great!" Butch said eagerly, and hurried to the foot of the stairs.

"What's that on the side of your head?" I asked as I followed him.

"What?"

"That thing on the side of your head."

"This?" he said, touching a large swelling that looked as if it would make his flesh pop out from under his hair. "I fell skating."

"Your parents let you skate?"

"They let me join a hockey league!"

"I hate this room," Spike sighed as he threw himself down on my bed. "It's so girlie."

"Why?" I asked angrily. "Because you can walk through it? Because the bed's made?"

"No, because the bedspread matches the curtains and there's a photograph over there of you with your parents. You have a blotter on your desk, Jasper! A blotter! And what's that on your bookshelf? Is that a set of those *American Girls* books? My sister would love to move in here," Spike jeered.

I tried to control myself and ignore him but couldn't manage it for long. "That's the *Great Moments in Science* series," I said angrily. "And there are maps on the walls, in case you haven't noticed. Those are guy things. And look . . . look at this stuff on my bookshelf. Leather crafts. I have a merit badge in leather crafts from Scouts. *Boy* Scouts."

"But the room's painted pink," Butch said, as if that clinched it.

I tried to sound as if I didn't know what he was talking about. "Are you color-blind or something? These walls are tan."

"Color-blind?" Butch repeated. "I'd have to be blind as a bat to think these walls are tan. Barbie's Playhouse isn't as pink as this room."

"The paint can said tan," I complained. "What was I supposed to do when the room turned out like this?"

"Move out," Spike suggested.

"So what did you want me to look at?" I snapped at him. It was a sudden change of subject, but it worked.

He handed me two issues of *Weird News*.

"I'll leave you one if you want, but you have to give it back."

I started to thumb through the top copy. "That's okay. You can take them both with you."

"Your family gets this, too? Good."

"Actually, Spike, I've only seen this in the grocery store."

"I told you so," Butch called from where he was poking around in my closet.

"Then you'd better look at it carefully," Spike instructed me. "It's full of tons of great stuff we can use in the literary magazine."

I finished looking at the pictures in the first copy of the paper and started leafing through the second. "I'm not sure I understand what stories about people with extra ears growing out of their belly buttons or armpit hair so long they can curl it have to do with our school literary magazine."

Butch's voice floated out of my closet. "I told you he wouldn't."

Spike jerked upright on my bed. "Don't you see the possibilities? We could do stories on teachers at Teddy E. who have had Bigfoot's baby, janitors named Elvis, cafeteria cooks who are government scientists conducting secret experiments on Tater Tots . . . I got a million ideas from that paper."

"But none of those things are true," I objected.

"It's a *literary* magazine. The stuff in it doesn't have to be true."

"But it's not supposed to be weird, either. It has to be . . . you know . . . literary."

" 'Literary' is not supposed to mean boring, you know. You're not going to let me do anything for this magazine, are you?" Spike demanded.

I didn't want to, no.

"Your ideas—"

"Are too cool? Are you afraid someone might actually read the magazine if I'm involved with it?"

"That's not it."

"Then what is it?" Spike demanded.

"There is no 'it.' Your ideas just haven't been right."

"I had a whole magazine full of right ideas. I could put out a magazine myself with all the good ideas I had. I could do that, you know."

Butch came out of my closet holding my favorite blue shirt. "Look what I found! It's that old geezer shirt Jasper was always wearing to school at the beginning of the year. He keeps it on a hanger." He laughed and waved the shirt in the air trying to get Spike's attention. "It looks like something somebody's grandfather would wear to play golf."

"Ours wouldn't," Spike said without looking away from me.

"Oh, I don't know. He might if he wasn't dead."

I stepped across the room and wrestled Butch for my shirt.

"Okay! Okay!" I said, hoping Spike would go away if he got what he wanted. "The 'Top Ten Worst Science Fair Projects' was okay. We'll use that."

"And what about the list of 'Field Trips in Hell' I collected during gym class? That was pretty funny."

"Well, yeah. It was. But it wasn't finished. Are you going to finish it?"

"Of course I'll finish it."

"When?"

"Sometime."

"Spike, the deadline is the day before February vacation."

108

"That's forever."

"What about that story about somebody finding a time capsule in the school building? That was your best idea. Can you have that done, too? *And* spell-checked? We can't accept anything late from even one person or we'll have everybody turning things in late."

"Dream on, Jasper. There aren't going to be that many people who want to see their name in this thing. But don't worry. I'll get it to you in plenty of time."

That seemed to wrap everything up as far as I was concerned.

"Well, I have to put some time in on my science fair project," I said as I pulled a volume from *Great Moments in Science* off the shelf, let it open wherever it would, and pretended to be busy.

"What about a cover for the literary magazine?"

"What about it?"

"Ms. Spendolini asked me to make some cover designs for you la-de-dah editors to choose from," Butch said.

"She's been talking to you about the cover?"

She hadn't talked to *me* about the cover.

"Yeah. She likes covers that show action and show something that happened during the school year when the magazine was published, so it's like a souvenir."

I collapsed onto the chair next to my desk. Ms. Spendolini had told Butch what she liked.

"So," he continued, "I thought maybe we could show that car thief running through the cornfield on the other side of the vet clinic with the cops after him. That happened this year, and I'd only have to draw the tops of their bodies. The rest I could hide behind stalks of corn."

"At school, Butch! She meant things that happened during the school year at *school!*" I groaned. If only Ms. Spendolini would talk to me, *I* would understand her.

"Oh, yawn. Nothing ever happens at school. But what about the truck that caught on fire in the liquor store parking lot?" Spike asked Butch. "That would make a good cover, and you wouldn't have to draw bodies at all."

"Wow. Or . . ."

It was at that point that Mom came in with the ice cream and said it sounded as if we were all having a good time, and Butch and Spike said, yes, yes, we were. And they continued to have a good time just sitting in my room, eating my ice cream, and making lists on my paper of the past year's best local and national disasters. Meanwhile I accepted that they probably weren't going to go anywhere for a while and that I probably wasn't going to get anything done that afternoon and that train wrecks and robberies at the mall would probably never interest me the way they did them.

The next thing I knew, I was looking down at my desk. *Great Moments in Science* was still lying open, just as it had been ever since I'd pulled it off the shelf. The great moment on the page in front of me was on someone named Fleming, Alexander.

Eight

It Was Not What
I Would Have Done

Mrs. McNulty says it's the perfect science fair project," I told Lyddy as we were coming in from recess after school had started again. "The display of mold at various stages of growth will be very specific, others should be able to duplicate the experiment, and . . ." I paused dramatically. ". . . the part about Alexander Fleming will add a human touch."

Lyddy's response was disappointing. "Alexander Fleming?"

"The guy who discovered penicillin in a dirty old dish he'd left on a chair while he was on vacation," Butch explained as he threw his wet socks into the bottom of his locker and replaced them with a stiff, dry pair he'd found there.

I shouldn't have been surprised that Butch knew about Alexander Fleming. Butch had had a number of infected wounds over the years, and he knew a lot about antibiotics just from experience.

"The science fair isn't until May," Donny said. "Your project's already done?"

"Not done, but planned. Mrs. McNulty says planning is the finest research tool ever invented."

"And you say you found out about this person by accident in a book you just happened to have?" Christine said. "And *he* found penicillin by accident in a dirty dish he just happened to have? And . . ."

I saw the point she was getting around to making, and I didn't like it. I had been working on my science fair project for months. It was *not* an accident. Finding the Alexander Fleming article was . . . something else.

"What about your ceramic garden figure for Teddy Scholars? Did you finish that over vacation?" Lyddy asked.

"Yup."

"Darn. The glaze cracked on mine and I had to start over. I wrote my mythology skit, though."

"So did I."

"And how did *you* spend *your* Christmas vacation, Spike?" Spike asked an empty spot in front of his locker. Then he went and stood in it so he could answer himself, "Why, thank you so much for asking. I went skiing, I went to the movies, I played some new computer games, I—"

"We get your point, Spike," Lyddy said.

". . . read three *Star Wars* books, I finished a home

page for my mother's English class (which I got paid for doing, by the way). Let's see . . . oh, yes, I copied the Metallica CD I got for Christmas onto a cassette tape for Butch . . ."

We were interrupted by a cry from our classroom. When we got in we saw that Mrs. McNulty had done a cubby check while we were at lunch and recess. The possessions of those who hadn't made the grade had been dumped onto the floor. Donny, Christine, and two of our other classmates were on their knees.

"My, my, my. Did we have an earthquake?" Lyddy asked glibly. Her treasures were still where she'd left them that morning.

"Cubby checks come when you least expect them," Mrs. McNulty explained without looking up from the magazine she was reading at her desk. "Maybe by the middle of June you people will have learned your lesson. Do you think anyone's going to beg and plead with you to clean up after yourselves and take care of things next year when you're at the middle school? No way! If you don't take care of your things properly next year, they will be out of there! Gone!"

Butch crouched down and started to sort through his stuff, which really had scattered across an impressively large area of the floor. He had had a wide array of charcoal, drawing, and colored pencils in his cubby as well as every imaginable kind of crayon, an almost full vial of glitter, half a dozen glue sticks, two overdue library books, four brand-new erasers, a paper punch, three pairs of scissors, a handful of candy wrappers, and a partially eaten cupcake. He was making progress on the job when he became totally engrossed in admiring old art projects he'd stored in there and forgotten about.

It was a while before he noticed his cousin calling him from the end of the row of cubbies. He didn't look up until Spike gave him a well-placed nudge with his foot.

"Come see if you can fix this," Spike ordered.

Butch rushed along on his knees to a spot on the floor where Spike and Christine were huddled over what was left of a ceramic cup Christine had been using as a pencil holder.

"My uncle brought it back for me from Mexico," she explained to Butch. She was trying not to cry.

We all knew the cup, a hideous yellow-and-brown misshapen glob that no one else would have cried over. Once Butch said that if it had been his he would . . . Then he'd stopped and said it would never have been his because he'd never have anything so ugly.

"Do you think you can fix it?" Christine asked him.

"Well," Butch said, considering, "it's never going to hold water again. But if you're just going to use it for a pencil holder, I might be able to patch it together."

Christine smiled and sighed gratefully. "Thank you."

Girls didn't often smile at Butch, unless he was leaving a room, of course. You could just tell as he knelt to start piecing the cup back together that he was feeling pretty pleased with himself.

"Listen," he said, "in about five years I'll have a driver's license. Do you think you'd like to go out with me sometime?"

"It depends on where you want to go," Christine replied.

Mrs. McNulty called, "Get those things cleaned up off the floor before class begins or I'll get a janitor in here to clean them up for you."

"She violated your civil rights," Spike hissed to Butch and Christine. "You can have McNutty arrested for that, you know. And then after you've had her arrested, you can hire one of those lawyers you see on television and *sue* her."

"Sue a teacher? Way cool!" Butch laughed.

"Wouldn't that cost a lot of money?" I asked as I looked down at Butch's art supplies. I couldn't help myself. I had to get down on the floor and organize them.

"We could make her pay for the cup," Spike explained.

"But the cup only cost a few dollars, and lawyers charge a lot."

"The cup may have cost only a few dollars, but it came from Mexico, Jasper," Christine said huffily.

"We'll ask for money for psychological damages," Spike insisted. "It's very distressing to find your cubby empty. It's like breaking and entering. Butch may never be able to hold a regular job because of what happened here this morning."

"I never expected him to hold a regular job anyway," Lyddy announced on her way to her seat.

Spike picked up a stray pencil that had been rolling on the floor and snapped it in two.

"Hey! That's mine!" Donny complained.

"She makes me so damn mad!" Spike said through gritted teeth.

"All right, then. You can keep it."

Spike held one of the ends of broken pencil in his fist and began bashing it against the floor.

"Would you stop that?" I whispered while checking to see if Mrs. McNulty had looked up. "She'll send you out in the hall or give you recess detention."

"I'm not afraid of her!"

"Calm down, Spike. She's not the only teacher who does cubby checks."

"She's the only teacher who dumps stuff on the floor when kids aren't in the room. She's the only teacher who breaks stuff. Do you think that's right?"

He had me there. "But Christine knows how Mrs. McNulty is. It's not the first time she's dumped some- one's stuff on the floor. If she'd kept her cubby clean, Mrs. McNulty wouldn't have done anything to it."

"You wouldn't be saying that if it was something of yours that had been broken."

I had the good sense not to store anything in my cubby that could break, and I didn't think anyone else should, either. I didn't bring up those points because reason often doesn't seem to have much appeal for Spike under the best of circumstances, and he has no use for it at all when he's mad.

"Mrs. McNulty loves you, so you're safe from her. Everyone else is on their own, right?" Spike demanded.

"What do you expect me to do?" I asked.

"You could do something . . . if you wanted to."

"I can't think of anything."

Spike scowled over at Mrs. McNulty, who had put down her magazine so she could enjoy the scene she'd created. "I can."

"Some of you are going to be very disappointed with the report cards you'll be receiving in a couple of weeks," Mrs. McNulty began once she had called the class together for the afternoon. A big grin started to spread across her lipless face. "That's exactly as it should be. I hope you'll learn a little something from the experience. I hope you'll learn a little something about me. I have standards—just like the teachers at the middle school. We have standards and we maintain them no matter what."

She smiled down at Butch and Spike. "You don't have standards for yourselves? That's okay. But I'm not going to lower mine."

She looked at a girl in the third row. "You think you

don't have to care about school because you're going to grow up to be Miss Universe? Dream on. I have no illusions."

She shook her head sadly over Christine. "You're just waiting to get out of school so you can get a job waiting tables or driving a bus? I understand that.

"But you must all understand something. This classroom is mine, and this school year is all about me and my standards. Those of you like Jasper and Lyddy and a few others who have shown a willingness to follow my lead are going to leave here prepared to fit in at the middle-school world. Those of you who haven't . . . Well, I really don't know what's going to happen to you next year."

That thought didn't seem to trouble her much.

Mrs. McNulty was able to quiet down a group of kids faster than any teacher I'd ever had. But we were more than just silent right then. Bodies can stop moving, and that's one kind of quiet, but what happened to the kids in our class was something else. It was as if Mrs. McNulty had flipped a switch and turned us off. Our classroom was silent the way a house is silent when the electricity is suddenly and unexpectedly cut off because a car has hit a pole or lightning has struck a transmitter.

"Yes, Spike. I see you have your hand up. You have something to say?" Mrs. McNulty asked. She was still smiling, and her voice had a kind, unnatural tone that made me shift anxiously in my seat.

"Can I ask you a question about the middle school, Mrs. McNulty? It's something I've been worried about."

"Certainly." Mrs. McNulty sounded encouraging, but she looked wary.

Spike's face wore the sweetest, most innocent look I'd ever seen there. This is going to be bad, I thought. Real bad.

"I've heard that at the middle school boys have to wear athletic supporters to gym class. Do you know if that's true?"

There were a few nervous coughs and giggles.

"I don't know," Mrs. McNulty said through clenched teeth.

Spike looked over at Butch, and Butch's arm shot up in the air. "If it is true, do you know how we would find out what size we wear?"

Whoops and hollers filled the room. Mrs. McNulty started shouting, "Silence! Silence right now!" and threw open the door so she could send the Cootches and four or five other boys out to the hallway.

"Can I have a pass to the nurse's office?" Butch sobbed through the doorway. "I've busted my gut laughing!"

"To the office! All of you! Get down to the office this minute!" Mrs. McNulty roared.

We could hear doors opening and other teachers out in the hallway trying to find out what was going on. The noise Spike and his party were making was so bad we could still hear them when they made the turn into the wing where Ms. Spendolini's office was located.

Everything that happened in that room was the kind of stuff that gets talked about at school. But when the story was told hours and days and weeks later, it wasn't told as "The Legend of Mrs. McNulty's Cubby Check" but as "The Legend of the Cootches' Jockstraps."

It was not what I would have thought of, and it was not what I would have done. But, then, I wouldn't have done anything.

Nine

Except for You

The Monday after February vacation Lyddy and I were released from class while Mrs. McNulty was doing a penmanship exercise so we could spend a half an hour working with Ms. Spendolini on the literary magazine. It was our first editorial meeting.

At last.

All the way to the office Lyddy complained about Butch. Butch ignored her suggestions, he was too lazy to cheat (and she'd been watching), he was always wiggling around, he hid magazines in his social studies book so Mrs. McNulty would think he was studying, and he finished his spreadsheet the first day our group used the computer lab so he could spend the rest of the week playing with the art and design programs, which made her really, really mad.

"All the other teachers let their students move to new seats almost every month, you know."

"I know," I said.

"Well, I think it stinks that I've had to sit with him all year. It just stinks," she repeated as we entered Ms. Spendolini's office.

Ms. Spendolini looked up from a table and smiled. "Something stinks?"

Lyddy paused for just a second and then said, "Well, as long as you ask, yes, something does. It's the middle of February, and I've been sitting next to Butch Couture all year."

"I know. I see you there whenever I observe your classroom."

"Jasper has been sitting next to Butch and Spike all year, too."

"I know, Lyddy. Everyone in your room has been in the same spots all year."

"*And* every time we have to do a group project, we have to do it with the same people."

"Really? Well, you must all be very good friends by now."

"Good friends?" Lyddy said, horrified. "I'm in a work group with the Cootches! Both of them!"

"Really? Well, I've always thought they had some winning qualities."

What about me? I thought. I'm in Lyddy's work group. I have winning qualities.

A very serious and sincere look came over Lyddy's face. "Ms. Spendolini? Do you think you could talk to Mrs. McNulty about our seating arrangements?" she asked very politely. "You're the principal. I'm sure she'd listen to you."

"Oh, I'm sure she would, too. But the school has no official policy about seating arrangements in the class-room. Teachers have the right to make those decisions for themselves. A principal shouldn't interfere in that aspect of a teacher's job."

Lyddy opened her mouth to say something else, but Ms. Spendolini cut her off.

"Now, since you sit right next to Butch, do you know what happened to the sample cover illustrations he said he'd make for us?"

"He was showing them to everyone in the room before vacation," Lyddy said, sounding pouty.

"I can't find them," Ms. Spendolini sighed, looking over the hundreds of papers spread over her table. "And I wish we could have got Spike to write something for us."

"But he did," I told her. "He didn't finish it until just before the deadline, but he made it."

"Oh-oh. I wonder what else I've lost."

So did I. I stepped forward and picked up a picture of what looked like a horse with sticks for legs. "Maybe I could organize this for you, Ms. Spendolini. I could make you a system."

She looked at me and those beautiful lips of hers opened up into a huge smile. "Oh, I'd love that, Jasper."

It was the best half hour I had all that week.

• • •

We arrived back in our classroom in time to enjoy the last fifteen minutes of Mrs. McNulty's talk on the development of cuneiform writing. She was just explaining that the Code of Hammurabi was written in cuneiform when the bell for lunch rang.

The bad part about being chosen for special projects like the literary magazine or Teddy Scholars is that you miss things like that cuneiform talk.

"Okay, people, help me to remember where we left off when we begin social studies tomorrow," she ordered.

"I'll take care of that for you, Mrs. McN.," Spike offered. "Just leave it to me."

"Is it over yet?" Butch asked groggily as he lifted his head off his desk.

"Out of here," Mrs. McNulty ordered through gritted teeth.

"Butch? Spike?" I said hesitantly as they got up from their tables. "The things you submitted to the literary magazine . . . did you keep copies? I've read that writers always keep copies of their work," I explained to Spike, "and I was just curious . . ."

His eyes narrowed dangerously. "I just put it in the box on Mrs. McNutty's counter Friday morning. The deadline was Friday, so I made it. You lost it, didn't you?"

"I didn't. Uh . . . it was . . ."

"It was Ms. Spendolini," Lyddy broke in gleefully. She made a few kissing sounds. "She lost your work."

"Maybe Mrs. McNulty didn't turn the things in on Friday," I suggested. I went over to check the box.

"You people haven't forgotten the essays that are due Wednesday, have you?" Mrs. McNulty asked as she started for the door. Her voice was cheery. She didn't have lunch or recess duty that day. "Oh, come on! Did I forget to tell you? You're all going to write essays this week. Your topic will be 'The Scientific Method.' "

"What about it?" Spike asked.

"What it is, what it means to you, what it has to do with the science fair that's coming up shortly. Which reminds me, I have an exciting science fair update! I've found two experienced science fair judges. Real judges—not somebody's uncle who used to work for a company that designed toilets for space shuttles—" Mrs. McNulty broke off in mid-sentence when she noticed that I was over by the counter. "What are you looking for, Jasper?"

"Butch made three illustrations for the literary magazine, and Spike wrote a story. But we can't find them," I explained. "I was hoping they were here."

Mrs. McNulty stopped and sighed happily. "Ah, yes. The literary magazine. It's a great honor to be a published author or artist, isn't it?" she said as she went back to her desk.

Something about the tone of her voice made me very uneasy.

"And publication should be reserved for those people who are deserving of the honor, shouldn't it? I've decided that in my class the honor of publication will be bestowed upon those people who have earned it by making good grades."

As Mrs. McNulty made this announcement, she distributed papers to Spike, Butch, and two students at the back of the room.

"So," she concluded, "some of you didn't have your work turned in, in time for the deadline."

She stood in front of Butch and Spike and looked down at them.

"No amusing comments, boys? No jokes? Why don't I hear anyone laughing? Why, I *do* hear someone laughing! Me!"

She laughed all the way out of the room and down to the faculty lounge.

• • •

I got back from basketball practice that night and was just starting work on my Creating Music with Kitchen Utensils project for Teddy Scholars when Spike suddenly appeared in the doorway of my bedroom. I leaped out of my chair and clutched at my chest.

"Who let you in?" I cried, gasping for breath.

"Your mother. She said I could just come up."

What kind of mother let a Cootch into the house? I wondered.

Spike got right down to business. "What I need is to see some of the stories and poems and things that you guys have rejected for the literary magazine."

"Why?"

"Oh, don't worry. I'm not going to try to steal any of your dead pet stories or those lousy poems you guys are always printing about the Easter Bunny. I want to look at the cool stuff. I want the things you wouldn't publish because they told the truth and were about subjects the school doesn't want kids to think about like whether or not Hitler had any kids or what the words to the Macarena mean. You know, we really *are* going to have to wear athletic supporters next year in gym class. Do you ever hear a teacher at Teddy E. telling anybody about that? You do not."

He went on like that for a little while, suggesting that Lyddy and I were suppressing short stories and essays written by kids at Teddy E. about what *really* happens to the items in the lost-and-found box in the school office, who *really* shot John F. Kennedy, what *really* goes on at Brownie troop meetings.

"And if I give you a poem on athletic supporters what are you going to do with it?" I finally asked.

"Publish it," he announced gleefully. "There was an article in my sister's *Seventeen* about a girl who had her own 'zine. It told exactly how to do it."

I would have liked to have known just how often Spike read his sister's copies of *Seventeen,* but he was already excited enough without me ticking him off like that. So instead I asked him why he was doing it.

127

"Because McNulty doesn't have the right to hold back our stories and pictures."

I thought he was going to get started on civil rights again. "You mean because you have a right to free speech under the First Amendment to the Constitution?"

"The what to the what? Stick to the subject, would you? I mean the literary magazine has nothing to do with Mrs. McNulty. Teachers aren't supposed to use it to punish kids. And they're not supposed to smile when they punish you. It's not supposed to make them happy."

"If you didn't give her so many reasons to punish you . . ."

Spike threw his hands up in disgust. "Of course! *I'm* to blame. Just like Christine was to blame when Mrs. McNulty trashed her things and broke her cup. Just like Lyddy was to blame when Mrs. McNulty embarrassed her over a stupid Halloween party. Just like all those little kids in the cafeteria are always to blame when Mrs. McNulty drags them away from their tables and makes them sit by themselves."

A horn started blowing out in the driveway.

"Ah, geez. That's Pam."

Spike started to open my window. "You have something you don't want I can throw at her?"

"No!"

Spike leaned out into the dark. "Shut up out there!"

He pulled his head back into my room. "McNutty thinks she's stopped us. She thinks she's made us feel

128

bad. We're going to get published anyway, and we're going to feel great about it. And we'll give a break to a select few of the literary magazine submissions that are too good for you guys to publish."

"I'm not going to give you any of the stuff from the literary magazine," I said.

"What about cash then? My father and uncle will do the photocopying at their offices, but we have to pay for the paper. I bet your grandparents gave you money for Christmas. Do you still have any?"

"You are out to get a teacher, and I'm having nothing to do with it."

"She's out to get us!" Spike wailed.

"She's not out to get me. In fact, she's always been very nice to me."

"Are you kidding me? Nice to you? Mrs. McNulty has had you sitting between Butch and me all year because you were the only kid there she knew would do only what he was told, who would never be tempted to have a good time. You're there between us to help keep us in line. You're there to make her job easier. She's had you in the hot seat all year long. And you think she's nice to you? Everyone thinks you're so smart, Jasper. But how smart can you possibly be when you don't understand something like that?"

"You think you're so smart," I said angrily, "but how smart can you be if you think I'm going to help you? What you're planning isn't right, Spike."

Pam started in with the car horn again and Spike darted into my closet to grab something he could fling out the window. One of my good church shoes went sailing out into the night and, from the sound of it, hit a hood dead center.

He closed my window with a crash and turned back to me for one last shot before he stormed out of my room.

"You wouldn't know what's right if it jumped up and bit you on the butt."

· · ·

It had taken Butch and Spike five and a half months to come up with ideas for and complete their contributions to the *Theodore Ervin Memorial Elementary School Literary Magazine*. It took them just a few weeks to churn out hundreds of copies of *West Adams Uncensored*. They were being passed around the playground after lunch one day when I got to recess late because I'd had band practice.

West Adams Uncensored

Everything the Folks at Teddy E. Don't Want You to See

$ .25 Vol. I. Iss. I March 8, 1998 $ .25

Publishers:	**Butch and Spike Couture**
Coeditors:	**Spike and Butch Couture**
Story Eds.:	**Butch and Spike Couture**
Associate Eds:	**Spike and Butch Couture**

Publishers' Statement

Welcome to the first issue of *West Adams Uncensored,* West Adams's first and only underground magazine—underground meaning old coots have nothing to do with it. We created *West Adams Uncensored* so that the people of this town could read the good stuff that the Teddy E. literary magazine won't publish because it's too interesting for them.

REGULAR FEATURE:
Stories Teachers Wouldn't Submit to the Teddy E. Literary Magazine Because They Were Too Good

---

This issue: "Time Capsules Give Insight into Childhood as It Was Lived in the Distant Past"
by Spike Couture

Oct. 31, 2050. The eagerly awaited demolition of that hideous and dangerous eyesore, the Teddy Ervin Elementary School, was a real boon to this community. Not only did it provide West Adams with a lovely new spot for a garbage transfer station and recycling plant, but, in addition, seven time capsules were found while the nuclear-powered backhoes were digging out the foundation.

The time capsules date from the late twentieth century, when children suffered horribly at the hands of their teachers. They give us new information as to what these poor little things were forced to do.

The capsules cover seven consecutive years. The same names are mentioned over and over again, so we come to know and pity these little people. It is so sad. So sad.

The children's story begins when they were five or six years old. They were forced onto large yellow vehicles by their parents and shipped to the forbidding Teddy E. building, where they were herded, sixteen or seventeen at a time, into rooms where there was nothing to sit on but little tiny chairs. Sometimes they were expected to sit on little squares of carpet on the floor. For more than two hours they were made to clap their hands and sing pointless songs about spiders that climbed up waterspouts and then turned around and climbed back down. They were force-fed raisins and unsalted popcorn and dry crackers. All they were allowed to drink was unsweetened juice. Over and over again they had to write their names in big letters with crayons so huge they could hardly get their little hands around them. They weren't allowed to go to the bathroom whenever they wanted to, and one little boy named Donny wet his pants three times. When they grew tired, they were prodded and poked into wakefulness. A little girl named Christine hid in a torture chamber referred to as "the playhouse" on two different occasions, so she could take a nap.

At the end of the year they were dressed up in goofy hats and had their pictures taken. They were told they were graduating into first grade.

It was all a trick, a horrible, horrible trick.

The hideous songs ended in first grade, but then reciting the alphabet began. They were forced to decipher marks on paper that meant things like "Pat had a cat" and "We went on a sled." There were other marks that had even less meaning. Nowadays no one would dream of asking anyone under the age of eighteen to try to explain 1 or +.

The year called second grade was when they began writing about what had happened to them in little books called journals. But since they spent most of their day at Teddy E., nothing happened to them and they had nothing to write about. A little boy named Butch used to draw pictures in his journals. The teacher (the name given to the person in charge of his torture) sent a note to his parents saying he needed special help. Another boy named Spike used to make things up to write in his journals. He was punished for using up too many books.

By third grade most of the children could read quite well. Instead of being rewarded, the torture took on a new form—they were made to read awful stories about the food grown in South Carolina in 1759 and the water cycle. There were beautiful books all around the room, but the children weren't allowed to read them. The books were just there to torment them.

The devils who ran the school thought of more evil to force on the kids in fourth grade—they made them study a foreign language and begin doing scientific experiments.

There were field trips every

year. Perhaps one hundred children at a time would be herded onto buses and driven to some place where they were shepherded around in groups by adults who yelled at them the entire time. Then they would be driven back to school, where they were told they should be grateful for the awful time they'd had.

As the children got older, not only were they tormented during the day, but they were given work to take home so their parents could continue tormenting them in the afternoon and evening. In fifth grade this aspect of the torture became particularly painful, with some children having to do as much as fifteen or twenty minutes of this so-called homework each day. By this age, some of the children's minds had become so twisted by what they'd had to endure that they would voluntarily do two or three hours of this unnatural work. Those children were called Teddy Scholars.

By sixth grade most of the children were zombies, walking dead. It wasn't much fun for the adults to persecute them anymore, so they had to introduce something new—stories about something called the middle school, which was supposed to be the next place where the children would be imprisoned.

The capsules end there. All we know of the middle school are the frightening descriptions of lack of food and filthy toilets. What it actually was like we can only imagine—if we dare.

REGULAR FEATURE:
Boy in the Bathroom Interview

This issue's question: "If you had to be trapped on an uninhabited island with one Teddy E. teacher, who would you choose?"

Donny: "Mr. Marlin because he is a war hero and a gym teacher, and so we'd have a good chance of living if he was there."

Butch: "Mr. Marlin because he knows how to shoot a gun, and I think he has one, too."

Peter: "Ms. Spendolini because she is a leader, and every group needs a leader." (yuck)

Kevin: "Mr. Marlin."

John: "I wouldn't want any of them because I wouldn't want to share my food and water with them. That would be my best chance of surviving."

Anonymous: "Mrs. McNulty because she is so mean. Only the good die young, you know."

We know!

REGULAR FEATURE:
Literary Magazine Rejects

The following pieces were rejected by the coeditors of the Teddy E. literary magazine. They are obviously class assignments from some first- and second-grade teachers who then forced these kids to turn their work in to the literary magazine.

The editors of *West Adams Uncensored* like the first piece because it is short and to the point. Some of these teachers overdo the "more details" stuff in our opinion. We just plain liked the second piece.

Send us your rejected literary submissions (or homework papers) for future issues.

My Favorite Animal
My favorite animal is the horse.
—*Roberta Covy*

Spring
Sap
Puddles
Rubbers
Ick
Nose Colds
Grass
—*Brendan Gates*

SPECIAL FEATURE:

The Truth About Middle School
by Doug Couture

The pleasures of middle school are among the best-kept secrets in West Adams. I've done six years of grade school, two years of middle school, and three and a half years of high school, and I can say without hesitation that middle school was the high point of my educational experience. My older brother, who's a sophomore in college, agrees with me.

There are so many marvelous things about middle school that it's hard to pick just a few to write about. But, of course, I have.

The most obvious difference between grade school and middle school is that you have a different teacher for every subject. Yes, that means a lot of running around from class to class. But it also means a lot of running around from class to class! In addition, if you end up with a feeble teacher (and you will), you won't have to spend more than forty minutes a day with him or her.

Second, nobody really gives a damn what you do there. There are rules for absolutely everything, of course, but you are expected to obey them without a great deal of nagging and coaxing. No one will complain to your family about the things you do, either. There will be no trouble of any kind until you flunk a subject or get kicked out of school.

This is freedom, and it is good.

The world of physical education changes dramatically when you get to middle school. In a word—showers.

And all the stories you've heard about what the cafeteria is like at lunchtime? They're all true. You're going to love it!

I often wish I were in sixth grade again and getting ready to go off to middle school. Instead, I am in twelfth grade and getting ready to go off to college.

I understand I have a great deal to look forward to there, also.

In conclusion, I would like to thank my younger brother and my cousin, Butch and Spike Couture, for honoring me with this invitation to write for the inaugural issue of their new publication, *West Adams Uncensored*. Congratulations and good luck (you're going to need it).

REGULAR FEATURE:
It's Just My Opinion, But . . .

This issue: "Why Isn't There a Student on the School Board?"

by Butch Couture

Whenever something rotten happens at Teddy E., like having to take Spanish or having to use those awful social studies books or the new fifteen-minutes-of-home-work-a-night rule in the second grade, we are told that the school board did it. The school board is responsible for everything that's wrong at Teddy E.

Did you ever wonder what this mysterious school board is? I did. I investigated the school board, and here's what I found.

In our town, there is a group of people who decides how much money the school can spend, who will be principal and assistant principal, and approves what will be taught. This group of people is called the school board. According to my source (my father), they are a bunch of old farts who haven't seen the inside of a school since the days when schools were heated with woodstoves.

How can these people possibly make decisions about what should go on in a school when they have no idea what goes on in one? In addition, they would make more reasonable decisions if their decisions actually affected them. If there was a student on the school board, there would be at least *one* person there who could tell the others what was really going on and who would have to face the consequences from the kids for the foolish decisions the school board makes. *Then,* we would see the school board acting with a little more care.

Write to the school board to let them know you want to see someone who knows what they're doing working with them.

"How did they get that stuff from the literary magazine?" I wondered aloud to Lyddy.

She stared at me with her eyes popping just a little and her mouth stretched into a nervous frown. It was her "I've been caught" look.

"Lyddy! Why? You can't stand Butch, and you don't like Spike."

Lyddy looked around to see if anyone could hear us. Then she whispered, "But I really, really don't like Mrs. McNulty. She's been horrid all year long, and I'm glad the Cootches have shown her that there are two people in this school she can't beat."

I looked over *West Adams Uncensored* again. "I suppose you must have typed it, too. Neither one of them can spell this well."

"Christine helped them. She can't spell to save her life, either, but she's willing to take the time to use spell check."

"You didn't give them money for paper, did you?" I asked.

"Oh, please! That was Donny. He only got two C's on his report card second marking period, and his parents were very generous."

"Gee. Everybody worked on this."

Lyddy nodded. "Except for you."

Ten

Deal with It

April Fool's Day fell on a Saturday, and I spent part of it in the Theodore Ervin Memorial Library finishing my research on Alexander Fleming. I was really excited about some stuff I'd just found when I noticed something moving at the other end of the research area. And then another something. And then I realized they weren't some*things,* they were some*ones.*

It's true what they say about bad pennies. They just keep turning up.

"Ask him," I heard Butch whisper.

"No. I won't talk to him unless he helps with the next *West Adams Uncensored.*"

"I don't know when the next *West Adams Uncensored* will be, but we're going to have to sit here for an hour and a half *today* if you don't ask him."

"You do it."

"No. It's your fault we're here."

"What do you want?" I finally asked.

Spike came closer to my table.

"How much longer are you going to be here, and how are you getting home?" he asked unpleasantly.

"My father's coming back to get me in twenty minutes."

Spike looked over his shoulder at Butch, who grinned and plopped down in a chair across from me.

"He'll be *happy* to give us a ride to my house."

That was all too true, I knew.

Spike sat down a little less eagerly and stared silently at my books and note cards—for about thirty seconds. That is what having Spike refuse to speak to you means. Pauses.

"What are you doing?" he asked.

"I'm working on my science fair project."

If I had sat down and tried to think of the worst possible thing to say, I would never have been able to come up with something that perfect.

"You don't *have* to take part in the science fair," Spike exclaimed wildly. "No one *has* to."

"I know." I just mouthed the words.

"It's still a free country, you know. It's not like we're living in a police state or something. Nobody—"

"Aunt Evie's making Spike do a science fair project," Butch said. "That's why Pam dumped us here."

I forgot myself and spoke a little too loudly. "You? You're doing a science fair project? Why?"

"Mmmmm, er . . ." Spike said vaguely.

139

"His parents got a letter from the school."

"Do you mind?" Spike snapped at his cousin.

I leaned toward Butch and whispered, "What did the letter say?"

"It was signed by Mrs. McNulty and a guidance counselor. It said he's at risk."

"At risk for what?"

"Spike won't say. But I know it involved low science and math grades."

"Did your parents get a letter, too?"

Butch nodded happily. "Guess what? I already know I'm going to pass sixth grade! The letter said I'm being recommended for two remedial classes at the middle school."

I caught a glimpse of Spike's face, and we both burst out laughing.

I managed to squeak out a "Congratulations, Butch."

"I know it's not a program for the academically gifted or anything, but I figure, hey, the pressure's off. I'm going to middle school."

Who would have thought Butch felt pressure about school? Or anything else, for that matter?

"For Spike, however, the pressure has just begun. Aunt Evie is ripping."

"Dad's mad, but my mother is out of her mind. And she's blaming me."

I thought that was very reasonable of her, but I knew better than to say so. I just muttered something like, "Go figure," and everyone quieted down so I could go back to work.

But not for long.

"What are all these little cards for?" Spike asked.

"Spike, we have to be quiet or one of the librarians will come over and complain," I warned.

"I hope it's not the one with the warts." Butch shuddered.

"None of the librarians have warts," I said as I bent down over my work again.

"The one who threw me out of here last summer sure did. Yuck!"

"So what's with the cards?" Spike asked again, pointing to my file box.

"Those are my notes," I explained. "I've got a bunch of cards for each book or magazine I read. I write one fact on each card. Then when I'm ready to do the written part of the project I'll lay the cards out into sort of an outline."

"Can't you remember anything?"

"It's science, Spike. You're supposed to be precise."

"Is that the word *mucus* I see on that card over there?" Butch asked eagerly. He picked it up and read out loud, "'Discovered a protein using a culture of his own nasal mucus.'"

"Isn't that disgusting?"

"Yeah!" Butch said appreciatively.

"So that's one fact about Alexander Fleming." I held

up the cards I'd completed just before I saw them. "Here's another about how sloppy he was. And another about how he didn't follow careful procedures. This guy had awful work habits, just awful. I don't think anyone would let him work in a lab today. Isn't it scary to think that we owe penicillin to someone who did everything wrong the way Fleming did? What if he had locked the cat in the lab with that culture dish he left on a bench while he was gone for a week? And the cat had eaten the mold? And . . ."

I could see the Cootches' eyes glazing over right in front of me.

"Penicillin meant the difference between life and death for thousands of people. Don't you get it?" I asked them excitedly. "It was all due to luck. He didn't plan what happened. People's lives shouldn't have to rely on things that aren't planned!"

A librarian came over and asked me to be quiet.

"Geez, Jasper," Spike said, loudly enough for her to hear as she walked away. "How could you embarrass us like that?"

I tried to think of something nasty to say. I thought, So what are you doing your project on? might do the trick. Any science project of Spike's couldn't be much.

"My mother thinks I should do something about how leaves produce food," he groaned.

"Ah, yes. Photosynthesis."

"Photowhat?"

"Photosynthesis," I repeated. "That's what it's called when plants produce food."

"Oh. Take one of his cards, Butch, and write that down."

"Why me?"

"You're supposed to be helping me, remember?"

"There's got to be some other way I can help," Butch said as he glumly went to work.

"So, Spike, I guess this letter your parents got means you're going to start studying now, huh?"

That was another nasty thing I thought of to say.

"I'm doing a science fair project to get my mother off my back. That letter was just McNutty's way of trying to make me miserable. If I start studying, she'll think it worked."

"Didn't it?"

He pointed a finger at me. "Spike Couture cannot be beaten."

I surprised myself by hoping that he was right.

• • •

"There are three basic rules for science fair projects," I explained during recess a couple of weeks later. My group had gathered around the old bench at the end of our playground. "First off, you can't kill anything."

I thought that was sort of dramatic, so I stopped to create a nice effect.

"Kill anything? Why do they have to have a rule like that?" Donny asked. Mrs. McNulty was holding a meeting in the gym before school ended that day for anyone interested in entering the science fair. He was hoping a science project would endear him to her in time to influence his final grades.

"Some people might want to dissect animals to show how organs work or something like that," Lyddy explained.

"Wow. I didn't know you could do science projects like that," Butch said.

"I just told you, you can't! There's a rule against killing things."

"What if you happened to just find something dead?" Butch wondered aloud.

I didn't think that was likely to happen, so I went on to the next rule. "You can't use human subjects."

"Didn't you just cover that in the first rule? What would you use people for other than dissecting?" Spike asked.

"You could test medicines or chemicals on them. Or you could feed one person one kind of food and another person another for a few weeks and see who does better. Except that you can't because there's a rule against it. There's also a rule against genetic engineering."

Christine sighed. "There was something about genetic engineering in a book I read. I skipped over it."

"Genetic engineering is cool. It's when you make something mutate," Spike explained.

"Like comic book heroes," Butch added. "I didn't re-

144

alize there were so many interesting things to do at science fairs—except there are rules against all of them."

"Now, there are three kinds of projects you can do," I said.

"Is that a rule?" Spike broke in. "You said there were only three rules, but this sounds like a fourth one."

"Look," I said impatiently, "I'd much rather be playing kickball. Do you want help getting started on science fair projects or not?"

"Not!" Butch and Spike shouted together.

"I do," Donny said. "I'm in the middle of baseball practice, and the season starts the beginning of May. I don't have a lot of time to work on a project. I've got to find an easy way to do this."

"Okay, then. There are three things people do at science fairs—"

"Including being bored to death?"

"Spike! Would you get out of here?" I demanded.

"No. This is too much fun."

"You can make a model of something, or you can display something you've learned about, or you can take a survey of something," I rattled off as quickly as I could. "Just pick one of those three things and do it."

"That's it. I give up," Christine said as she got up to go sit with some girls who were making barrettes and bracelets out of strips of plastic. "This is too much to go through for a project Mrs. McNulty won't like anyway."

"If you want to do well and win an award or something, you have to be specific," I called after her. Then I looked at Spike. "Say you're doing a project on photosynthesis—"

"Photowhat?" Donny asked.

"The process by which plants produce food," Lyddy explained.

"There's a subject I've always wanted to know more about," Butch said.

"Me, too," Spike agreed. "Why, just the other day—"

"If you are doing a project on photosynthesis," I repeated, "you can't just ramble on and on about every leaf on the planet. And try to be original. Try to find something new to say about photosynthesis."

Lyddy nodded her head in agreement. The others stared at us with their mouths open.

"If I come up with something new to say about photosynthesis, I better get something a whole lot better than a ribbon at a fair," Spike said as the bell rang.

• • •

Butch was sent out of the room twice that afternoon, and Spike even made it down to the principal's office, but they were both in the bleachers (on either side of me, of course) for Mrs. McNulty's meeting.

"Quiet! Quiet up there! Did I give you the impression that we have all afternoon to get settled? I'm sorry. We have to get started at exactly 2:30 if we're going to get out of here in time for the buses. And we *are* going to get out of here in time for the buses.

146

"Now Ms. Spendolini and I want to go over some changes in this year's fair. First off, there will be four awards per grade level—first, second, and third places, and honorable mention—and the same four awards for overall winners. No more ribbons for the *biggest* project or the *smallest* project or the *funniest* project or the *smelliest* project or any of that foolishness! Those days are over and good riddance to them."

A few groans and whispers rumbled around the gym.

"The biggest change, of course, is that I will not be judging it this year."

Some of the braver kids started clapping.

"We'll see if you're still applauding in May. Because I'm talking about *judges,* real *judges.* These people spend hours at science fairs. They see thousands of projects. Do you know what you're going to have to do to impress them? . . . Do you? . . . Neither do I! I don't know if they *can* be impressed. At the end of that science fair next month there are going to be a great many of you wishing you could turn back time to the days when a grade school teacher was handing out those awards."

"Not if the grade school teacher was McNutty," Butch whispered.

"Let me give you a word of advice. The best way to prepare for those judges is to plan. Always remember, planning is the best research tool ever invented! If that's the only thing you learn from this experience, I'll be satisfied!"

"The McNutt is *never* satisfied," Spike said.

"While you are doing your planning, remember the Scientific Method . . ."

"Remember it?" a kid sitting in front of us said to his neighbor. "I've never heard of it."

"All we're requiring you do to prove you understand the Scientific Method," she continued grimly, "is show us that you are familiar with the work of authorities in your field, show us you have observed something yourself, show us you have addressed your errors, and show us you have done something that can be duplicated by others."

Butch and Spike looked at each other and started to laugh.

"Like any of that's going to happen," Butch snickered.

Mrs. McNulty scowled up at them and brought her voice up a little louder. "Count your blessings that we're not at the middle school. Now, if we were the middle school, we could have a *real* science fair and make you include an experimental control. However, you're just kids, so this is the best we can do."

Someone started sniffing behind me as Ms. Spendolini stepped forward to speak.

"That's right. You are kids, this is elementary school, and we are going to have a fair! Fairs are fun. No one is going to force you to do science projects. No one is going to choose your topic for you. What we are going to do is open up the gym for you one evening so you can show us what interests you and you can spend an hour wandering around looking at what your friends have been doing. And, of course, there will be doughnut holes—hundreds of them! Maybe thousands!"

A cheer rose up from the bleachers. "Yes! Yes! Yes!"

"Ms. Spendolini! Ms. Spendolini! Can I bring my hamster?"

"My mother wants to know if acids and bases would be a good project. What are they?"

"I want to do something on motors. Would that be all right, Mrs. McNulty? Are motors scientific?"

"Mrs. McNulty? Kevin in Ms. Napolitano's room and I want to do a project on cloning. Would that be good?"

Ms. Spendolini was laughing at the uproar, but Mrs. McNulty had her hands up as if she were trying to hold everybody back. She only responded to the voice she recognized.

"Donny, Donny, Donny. Cloning is way, way over your head, dear. It involves cell duplication. You can't possibly understand that. Why don't you and your friend choose a topic that's more your speed. Say, how a light bulb works."

"We did light bulbs in kindergarten," Donny objected, but a little weakly.

"See? It will be a good project for you then. But, you know," she continued addressing everyone there, "you people who are in Teddy Scholars might consider suggesting the cloning idea to your advisor. It would be a good project for you."

I felt as if I'd just seen Donny drop down an elevator shaft. I almost shouted out his name, the way you would if you saw your friend disappear from sight. It's true we were a noisy bunch, but I don't think Mrs. McNulty had ever been with a group of kids she couldn't shout over. Everyone in the gym had heard her embarrass Don. There was no doubt about it.

Ms. Spendolini had one hand on her hip and just stood staring at Mrs. McNulty. Without taking her eyes off her, she raised her arms over her head and clapped her hands once to get our attention. Then she said, "You sixth-graders are going to be taking final exams for the first time this year. Any of you who enters a project in the fair, whether it wins a prize or not, will receive ten points toward your science final."

Then Mrs. McNulty looked as if *she* were falling down an elevator shaft. You didn't have to be much of a hand at lipreading to see Ms. Spendolini tell her, "Deal with it," before she turned and left the gym.

"Out of here!" Mrs. McNulty hollered. "Everyone! Go back to your classrooms and get ready to go out to the buses!"

We barely made it to our lockers in time to collect our things. Lyddy and I, having the most to pack in our school bags, were still there when everyone else had gone. Something about the way she was leaning against her locker struck me as odd. I looked over at her, and then I looked again.

"Lyddy!" The word came out in a whisper I was so shocked. "Are you crying?"

Stupid question. She was sobbing so hard she was having trouble catching her breath. Her long, straight blond hair was caught in her tears and even in her mouth as she bent over her bag and tried to load it.

"What's wrong. What's happened?"

"I can't talk now. The woman who stays at the house with me after school is on vacation, so I don't have a way to get home if I miss the bus. My mother can't leave the office to come get me."

"My mother will come get us if we miss the bus," I promised, hoping she would. "What's wrong?"

Lyddy began to cry harder. "I can't do that science fair project, Jasper! Not the way Mrs. McNulty wants it done. I'm doing a research project on digestion because I thought it sounded . . . sounded smart. I was just going to have pictures, maybe a model or something. Just what am I supposed to say I observed? And what kinds of errors am I supposed to address? Am I supposed to write out a description of every time I erased something?

"And what about next year? What's an experimental control? Do you have a clue? I don't. What are we going to do? What are we going to do, Jasper?"

I brought my hand up and let it hover over Lyddy's

shoulder for a moment before I decided that, yes, patting her was the right thing to do. Her hair stuck to my fingers like some kind of silky material that catches on your nails. I was afraid I would snag it and ruin it somehow.

She sighed wearily and bent to pick up her bag. "I'll figure it out. I always do," she said. She carried a big shoulder bag because she couldn't find a backpack large enough for the amount of homework she liked to do. It was heavy enough to pull her shoulder down and give her a lopsided look as she walked away from me. "I don't know when, though. I have a piano recital coming up soon besides the spring band concert, so I have extra practices for the next month. Karate meets three times a week, you know. I baby-sit every Tuesday night for three kids who expect stories and games, and they're up until eight-thirty. Eight-thirty! Do you know how old I was before I could stay up until eight-thirty? I have two baseball practices a week now, and there'll be two games a week starting in May. My mother insists I have to go to church on Sunday." She grunted as she shifted her bag from one arm to the other. "Sometimes I wish I could just lie on the floor and watch television."

"You don't *have* to do a science fair project," I said as I walked with her. "It's still a free country, you know. It's not like we live in a police state."

Lyddy laughed, and it looked as if her eyes were beginning to dry up. She didn't seem any happier, though.

"Of course, I have to do a science fair project, Jasper," she said. "So do you. We can't *not* do one."

Then she walked away toward her bus, and I thought, Donny's embarrassed, Lyddy's crying . . . That's them, not me. It doesn't have anything to do with me.

Eleven

What Was
the Right Thing?

Nothing could make Don feel bad for long during baseball season. It lasted only two and a half months, but since fourth grade it had been two and a half months during which he ruled the town of West Adams. And no one minded, no one was jealous. That was how good he was.

By the week before opening day I was feeling pretty good again, too. My third-quarter report card had been particularly impressive, though the literary magazine was almost finished I was still seeing Ms. Spendolini every couple of weeks, and somehow Dad had managed to get both Donny and me on the baseball team he coached. I went to bed Thursday night thinking, Yes, it is good to be Jasper Gordon.

• • •

"Joey Negrelli broke his leg skateboarding!" Donny yelled down the aisle of the bus as I boarded it Friday morning.

"Joey Negrelli broke his leg skateboarding," I told

Spike and Christine in the hall on the way to class the next morning.

"Hey, Andy Negrelli's older brother broke his leg skateboarding," Spike told Butch at the lockers.

"I had nothing to do with it!" Butch wailed. He had taken a lot of heat for breaking Andy's leg during a soccer match, and the news about Andy's brother triggered a flashback. "The Negrellis are all klutzes."

"So Joey Negrelli broke his leg skateboarding, huh?" Lyddy said, looking at Donny. "That means, of course, that first base is empty on the tournament team. Too bad you have to be thirteen to play on it, Don."

"I'm not thirteen now, but I will be during the season," Donny explained. He was almost drooling with excitement. The West Adams Tournament Team represented the town in both state and regional competitions. He had been waiting to play on it since we started T-ball in kindergarten. "My birthday is two weeks before the last game. They don't have anyone else. I wouldn't be taking a spot from any of the other thirteen-year-olds. So the coach says that if I do well at the tryout, they won't bother looking for anyone else."

Christine didn't think he should have to try out at all. "None of those kids on the tournament team are as good as you are."

Everyone has to try out for baseball teams," I told her. "That's just the way it is. When are you trying out, Donny?"

"That's a problem. Mr. Torres, the head coach, is getting married tomorrow afternoon. Then he's going to Hawaii for two weeks for his honeymoon."

"The first two weeks of baseball season? Couldn't he plan any better than that?" I asked.

Donny shook his head. "I would have. Anyway, my team has a game tomorrow morning. He's going to try to come by to watch me play. He said he'd call that a try-out."

"My team" was actually "our team." Our coaches liked to name their bands of players for themselves, so my father called ours "Gordon's Team." It was a classy name, much more dignified than "Bob's Base Monkeys," the name of the team we were playing the next day, the opening day of the season.

The eight-thirty game was just finishing up, and the players were tearing out of the dugouts so they could line up in front of the refreshment concession for lunch when I arrived at the park. I was in the in field warming up when I heard someone cry out from where our opposition was tossing balls back and forth.

"Butch?" I called to a uniformed figure clutching its back. "What happened?"

"I don't know," Butch groaned. "But I think I'm going to need a new kidney."

"You turned around and walked away while someone was throwing balls to you, didn't you?"

"Are you trying to blame me for getting hurt?"

How did "Gordon's Team" manage to get Donny, the most desirable kid in the league, while "Bob's Base Monkeys" got stuck with Butch, the league outcast? Dad said some of the other guys owed him favors. And as for Bob, well, his luck had just run out.

At the end of practice, Dad took the pitcher's mound and started lobbing balls to Donny so he could belt them, one after another, to the far end of the outfield.

Lyddy pulled her glove off as she walked in from third base. "Is your father hoping that with a little more practice Donny will be able to put one through the fence or something?"

I looked toward the bleachers. "I think he might be putting on a little show for Mr. Torres. Do you see him anywhere?"

Butch had hobbled up to join us, and the three of us studied the bleachers, which were filling up with parents, siblings, and an unusual number of the players who'd just finished the game before ours.

"Oh, my gosh! Oh, my gosh!" Lyddy exclaimed.

"Do you see him?"

"No! I see Mrs. McNulty!"

And there she was, making herself comfortable next to one of the school secretaries and a woman who volunteered in the Teddy E. library. They'd all brought lawn chairs that they had set up in the most inconvenient spot next to the bleachers.

"She's supposed to be a screamer," I said.

"I believe it. She's exactly the type who will coach the players from the bleachers. By the fourth inning she's going to be bellowing, 'What do you think you're doing out there—taking a nap?' and, 'Didn't anybody tell you guys you're supposed to *catch* the ball?' "

"I hope she does," Butch said enthusiastically. "My father is coaching first base for our team today. If she gets noisy like that while he's on the field, he'll pop her the bird."

We all agreed that was something we could all look forward to.

Dad and Donny finally left the field ten minutes after the game was originally scheduled to start. Dad was worn out from pitching, and Donny had lost two balls over the fence. Mr. Torres hadn't shown up to see any of it.

"Oh, well. It's just baseball," Donny said dejectedly sometime during the first inning after he'd hit a ball to the corner of the field, bringing three other players and himself home. He sat on the bench with a batter's helmet dangling limply between his legs.

"Just baseball?" Lyddy said as she took the helmet from him and started to pull it over her head. "Just baseball? You're almost thirteen, Donny. You've got to start thinking about your future. Does the expression 'sports scholarship' mean anything to you? How do you think people get those? Not by playing ball on a team coached by somebody's dad. You have to play in high school with real coaches. And you can only play in high school if you've been playing on the very best kid teams." She shook her head sadly. "This tryout could have been big for you, Don. It's too bad Mr. Torres didn't show. I've read that sometimes there are scouts for national kids' teams at some of the regional tournaments, and if you could only have got on the team maybe . . ."

"Lyddy? Perhaps you'd like to take a few practice swings over here behind the dugout," my mother, who was keeping track of the lineup for our team, suggested.

"Oh, sure, Mrs. Gordon."

Lyddy picked up a bat, tossed one of her braids over her shoulder, and headed out of the dugout.

"Oh, for the good old days when girls couldn't play on boys' teams," a voice said behind us.

"Spike? What are you doing here?" I asked.

I couldn't imagine him watching a sporting event on television, in the comfort of his living room, let alone from a bench out in the fresh air.

"My aunt asked my father and me to run the gas grill at the concession stand for her," Spike bragged. "You understand what that means, don't you? Nobody here gets a hot dog unless *I* say they get a hot dog."

"His uncle was going to do it, but he's coaching first base this morning. Thank goodness. It makes me nervous when Scooter lights a match, let alone a gas grill," a man who appeared to be with him said.

His hair was curlier than Spike's and much longer.

He'd pulled it back in a ponytail, which exposed his pierced ear. His hair and eyes were that same shade of brown as Butch and Spike's. They made me think of a pot of thick melted chocolate. Except that in the man's case, his hair was laced with white. And he had that wide mouth that you don't see on all that many people. He and Spike were wearing matching T-shirts, which would have been kind of dorky, except that they were so faded you could hardly read the message about road kill printed on them.

Spike directed our attention toward the man by pointing at him with his thumb. "My dad." Then he pointed at us and said to his father, "My . . . uh . . . uh . . ."

"Friends?" his father suggested.

"I guess."

Mr. Couture moved the spatula he was holding from his right hand to his left and reached into the dugout to shake hands with Donny and me. I couldn't remember ever actually touching a Cootch before.

"You guys are lucky to be here this morning." He smiled fondly. "I loved this place when I was a boy."

"Did you play baseball?" Donny asked. The presence of a Cootch father was helping him perk up a bit.

"Are you kidding? Hit a ball and run around in a circle? I don't think so. No, my brother was the ballplayer in our family. I used to come here and watch him play."

"Butch's father was an athlete?" I couldn't believe it.

Butch didn't act as if he'd ever even seen an athlete. How could he be related to one?

"Athlete? That's a good one. No, actually, he just *played ball.* All kinds of ball, though baseball was the only game I liked watching. In soccer and basketball you just run from one end of the court or field to the other. But baseball is a thinking man's game. I remember when Scooter broke his nose over by third base falling over a shortstop. He was stealing, of course. Stealing bases was his strong point. He was very clever about it. That's why I like baseball. Cleverness counts."

Mr. Couture turned his head, as if he were listening to something. A moment later we heard it, too: "Buddy! Hey, Buddy!"

Donny and I leaned out of the back of the dugout and saw a figure running toward us.

"I've been looking everywhere for you," he told Spike's father. "Do you have any money?"

This man I'd actually seen before, since he was an assistant coach. I'd never seen him the way I was seeing him right then, though.

"You're forty-two years old, Scooter. You're supposed to carry money with you—your own money."

"I left my wallet at home. It could happen to anybody." Scooter Couture's brown eyes looked startled—amazed—that anyone would suggest he wasn't totally innocent in this particular situation.

"How much do you need?" Buddy asked as he reached into his pocket.

"Nothing for me. But would you feed Butch? You know, just get him a couple hot dogs, maybe a hamburger and some chips? He brought ice water with him, but he'll probably want some soda. He always wants soda. And if he asks for candy or an ice cream bar, let him have it. He'll run it off." Scooter smiled at his brother, a smile that stretched right across his face.

"Didn't he eat lunch?" Buddy asked, frowning into his wallet.

"No, and he slept through breakfast. I'll pay you back tonight."

Then they turned their attention to Donny so Scooter could talk to him about the tournament team. I just stood there, silently staring at them. The eyes, the color of the hair, the wide mouths on the broad faces—they were all the same. Only the Couture adults looked even more alike than the Couture kids did. The lines around their eyes, the creases near their mouths, the breadth of their shoulders, the way they leaned and dipped their heads to talk to Don . . . everything was the same.

"I'm baby-sitting first base next inning, so I better go keep track of what's going on," Scooter finally concluded. "Don't worry, Don. Torres will show up any minute. The wedding is supposed to be around two-thirty or three. That's hours away."

"Spike," I said in amazement as we watched the two

men walk away, their strides equal, their shoulders held in exactly the same manner, their blue jeans hung from what seemed to be matching hips, "your father and your uncle are twins!"

"No!" Spike replied. "You sure?"

"How was I supposed to know? You never said anything."

"They're not just any twins. They're identical," he boasted.

"I've never seen twins who weren't kids before," Donny said, awed.

"Did you think they didn't grow up?"

"It must be so cool to have a twin," I said. I kept my eyes on the Couture dads as long as they stayed in sight.

Spike agreed. "I wish I had somebody I could borrow money from no matter where I was. I guess I better get to the concession stand before my father spends everything he's got on Butch. If he's missed two meals, he could end up eating all afternoon."

In fact, Butch was polishing off a bag of potato chips and a soda when he showed up at the top of the third inning.

"Hey, you guys are really pulling ahead of us now," he said.

"Butch, you shouldn't be here," Lyddy told him.

"Why not?"

"You are on the opposing team! You're supposed to stay with your own kind," she explained. "Your coach is going to have a stroke if he sees you've left your dugout and are wandering around."

"Ah, my coach has a stroke if somebody burps on base. I don't want to sit with my team. Everybody in my dugout is upset because we're losing. Coach just got through telling us we're playing like crap," Butch said.

They were, though I wouldn't have put it quite like that myself.

"You know, I'm only going to have to play two innings in the field and one up at bat," Butch told us. "But you guys have already had to play three in both places, and the game's only half over. You ought to talk to Jasper's father about the way he's organized your lineup. He's got you playing too much."

Donny laughed. "There is no such thing as playing too much," he said.

"Well, it hardly seems fair that you guys should have to play the whole game. I'm having a great time. I've had two hot dogs so far today and read a comic book somebody's little brother brought. Oh, and look! There's Chrissie and her brother! I'm going to go over and sit with them for a while. You guys ought to complain about Mr. Gordon," Butch called over his shoulder.

"You know," Donny said thoughtfully as we watched Butch join Christine near the bleachers, "I don't think Butch understands that he's only playing two innings because his coach is playing his best players the most and he isn't one of the best players. He's not even close."

"I think he should be told," Lyddy observed.

"Ah, why? He's happy not knowing," Donny said.

"I'd be happy if we told him."

I looked behind Butch and Christine at the bleachers and then quickly scanned the people standing along the fence. There was still no sign of Mr. Torres.

But Mrs. McNulty was heading right for us.

"I just had to come over here and wish you luck, Donny," she said when she reached the dugout.

"Thanks, Mrs. McNulty. Thanks for coming, too."

"Oh, I'm known for my love of baseball. I'm sure you'll agree it's the finest game ever invented. And I'm so happy for you. I'm always happy when one of my students who isn't . . . oh, say . . . really a student? . . . has something nice going on in his life even if it is only baseball. We can't all be successful in everything, now can we? So we should be grateful for what little victories we can win."

Mrs. McNulty reached into the dugout, grabbed Donny's arm, and gave it a little shake. "I am so glad you have baseball in your life," she said. "You may not be much of a hitter in the classroom, but it's nice to know that out here you can be a star, isn't it?"

There was an awkward pause before Donny finally said, "Yes?"

"Hit one out of the field for me, dear. I'm going to be rooting for all of you," she cried over her shoulder as she headed back to her seat.

Lyddy punched Donny in the chest with one finger. "You hit one out of the field *at* her," she ordered.

"Lyddy!" I warned. My mother was standing right behind us.

"Get her right between the eyes," Mom said without looking up from her clipboard.

During the fourth inning, I got up to bat and let two balls go by.

"You gotta swing at 'em!" someone screamed from the bleachers.

The next ball was outside, and I ignored it.

"Take a chunk out of it!"

I stood at the plate and tried to keep my eye on the pitcher's hand. But there was so much space all around me and so many places for a ball to go where I couldn't get at it.

"You're a hitter, Gordon!"

Oh, please, just let this be over with, I thought as I took a beautiful chop at nothing.

"And just what was that supposed to be?"

Mrs. McNulty was standing in front of her chair, shaking her head in disgust as she raised a bottle of Gatorade to her mouth.

"I'm glad she was rooting *for* you," Lyddy said just before I collapsed onto the bench.

We were just taking our positions on base for the second half of the fifth inning when I saw Spike running along the outside of the chain fence that surrounded the playing field.

"He just got here," he shouted.

"Mr. Torres? There's only an inning and a half left!"

"And it can't get over too soon, if you ask me. It's getting hot in those bleachers. Make this inning fast so we can get out of here," Spike ordered.

It was. Donny plucked the first hit right out of the air at first base and that was the end of that play. The second man up hit his second ball to Lyddy, who was shortstop. She sent the ball to Donny at first long before the batter got there. Butch was the third man up. I expected a strikeout or maybe a pop foul that would be caught by our catcher. But he had been getting plenty of rest in his dugout, when he wasn't over in the opposing team's bragging about how much candy and soda he'd packed away, and managed to hit a low ball off toward third. By the time the ball got to Donny at first, Butch should have been safe. But instead of staying put, he kept on going. His father did everything but grab Butch and hold him at first base. But nothing could stop him. He raced the ball to me at second.

"Slide! Slide!" the crowd in the bleachers screamed as both Butch and the ball headed right for me.

Butch slid, and I held my ground.

When the dust settled, I was holding the ball on base with Butch's arms wrapped around my feet.

"Damn it, Butch, if I've told you once I've told you a hundred times," his father hollered. *"Not head first."*

Butch bounded to his feet, and if it hadn't been for the blood gushing from his mouth, I would have sworn he was just fine.

Soon we were surrounded by both Couture dads, Butch's head coach, and my mother, who was pulling on a pair of latex gloves.

"Oh, this most definitely means a trip to the emergency room," she announced as she peered into Butch's mouth. "His braces are caught on the tissue on the inside of his mouth."

By that time Butch's pants and even one of his cleats were stained red. His face was growing paler, as if the blood were draining out of it. Which it was.

" 'ive o' 'ix 'uar's o' 'ood in a 'uman," he observed.

"You have to be down at least a pint, Butchie boy," his father speculated.

"I don't know," his uncle Buddy said. "A pint is only two cups. Could two cups make a mess this big?"

Buddy and Scooter looked at each other. They had the same look on their faces, and I could tell that they were having the same thought at the same time and they were sharing it somehow.

"Give him some ice to suck on and send him back to the dugout. He'll keep for another inning. Let's play ball!" Scooter shouted as he ran back to first base.

The coaches agreed to call Butch's double play safe

and allowed one of his teammates to take his place on second. This made it possible for Donny to tag the next batter at first and throw the ball home so the catcher could dispose of Butch's replacement before he got there.

"He's here," I whispered to Lyddy.

We had no difficulty finding him in the bleachers. He was the only short, bald man there with a thick black mustache and a tuxedo.

"What are you looking at?" Donny asked when he noticed them. "Mr. Torres! All right! How long has he been here?"

"Since the beginning of the second half of the last inning," I told him.

Donny grimaced. "I wasn't bad, but it wasn't exactly my best work, either."

We were way ahead, so Dad put one of the less able players into the batting order to give him a chance to play. He got a hit and made it to first base. The next person up, the last in the batting order, hit a triple play, which got the first man home and left him on third. Then we started at the top of the batting order again.

"He says he has to leave soon." Spike was hanging in to the back of the dugout again. "Mr. Torres says he has to leave soon."

"Oh, no," Mom muttered as she looked at the clipboard. "We just started over and Donny's fourth in the batting order. There are two more players before him."

"So move him," Spike said. "What's the problem?"

"I can't. Only the head coach can do that. And if he does pull . . . let's see, who is it? . . . Andy Negrelli and Jasper, they won't be able to bat again this game. You can't get back in order the same inning you're pulled, and this is the last inning."

Andy and I agreed we'd both had enough of being up to bat for one day, and everyone started yelling to get Dad's attention. But he was deep in conversation with the third base coach.

"Go on, Andy," Mom ordered. "Hurry."

Andy ran out to the plate, struck at the first three balls that came over it, and ran back to the dugout.

"E's 'edding up off 'e 'eacher!" Butch reported. He had been running, which started a fresh flow of blood around the ice he was holding to his mouth.

Donny kicked a wall and threw his cap on the ground.

"DONNY! DONNY! DONNY!" the crowd began chanting.

I was holding a bat and ready to go. "We already have two outs," I wailed. "If I strike out, Donny won't get up."

"If you go out there, it won't matter what you do because Torres will be gone!" Spike shouted. "Let Donny take your place!"

"He can't!" Lyddy insisted. "He can't change the batting order! Players can't change the batting order! If Donny goes out there for Jasper, whatever he does won't count! It will be an automatic out."

"DONNY! DONNY! DONNY!"

170

"Donny only has to show this guy what he can do. So what if it doesn't count? You're already ahead 15 to 2 at the beginning of the last inning," Spike argued. "Give him the helmet, Jasper."

"But I'm not supposed to!"

"DONNY! DONNY! DONNY!"

"Come on, Jasper!" Spike yelled. "Do the right thing!"

Mr. Torres was standing on the ground, brushing off his pants and straightening his cummerbund.

What was the right thing?

"DONNY! DONNY! DONNY!"

"Okay, okay," I said as I ripped the batting helmet off my head and gave it to Donny. "One more out won't kill us."

"DONNY!"

Donny positioned himself over the plate with his bat well over his right shoulder.

"Back up!" the opposing team's coaches ordered. "He's a hitter!"

"Strike!" the umpire shouted as the first ball went over the plate.

"Ball!"

"Good eye," Dad said encouragingly.

"Back up!" The other team's coaches shouted again. "He's going to belt it!"

"Strike two!" the umpire called when Donny let the next ball go over the plate.

"What are you waiting for?" Mrs. McNulty roared. "Christmas?"

"Okay, Donny. You've built up enough suspense now. Swing at the next good-looking ball," Dad ordered.

The pitcher looked nervous. But he drew back his arm and with one smooth motion sent a ball through the air that looked perfect just as soon as it left his hand. I could tell Donny thought so, too, because his bat came back and then . . . and then . . .

And then he bunted.

The entire infield stood rooted to their positions while Donny ran to first base. When the shock finally wore off, the pitcher, catcher, and third baseman fell over each other trying to pick up the ball. Someone finally got it to second base but not before Donny had slid safely in.

The crowd clapped politely, but you could tell they were disappointed. The bunt was good strategically. It took the infield entirely by surprise. But did bunts lead to college scholarships?

Mr. Torres called Donny out of the dugout and kept his fiancée waiting while the two talked. When Donny came back, he was smiling.

"Thanks, Jasper," he said. "I got my spot on the tournament team."

"Donny, what were you doing out there?" I asked. "You could have sent that ball anywhere you wanted. Why did you bunt?"

"Because any fool can hit a ball to the far end of the

field," Donny explained as he picked up his glove. "I had to show I could think, too."

I followed his gaze into the crowd of spectators. Mrs. McNulty was sitting at the edge of her folding chair, staring out at us with her mouth open. She was squinting into the sun, too, so she was left gaping like a badly congested mole.

Or maybe it was just the look of a person who didn't care for what Donny had just shown us.

Twelve

This Is Wrong

I missed part of recess the next Monday because I was in the band room practicing my saxophone solo for the school district convocation. When I got out to the playground, everyone was already doing something. There is nothing worse than not having something to do or someone to be with at recess, and getting there late usually ensures that that's exactly how you'll be. I was afraid I was going to be stuck.

There was a crowd of boys and girls pretending to play red rover, so they could grab at each other in a manner that wouldn't embarrass anyone or bring a teacher racing over. The kickball field was occupied by a knot of boys like Butch, who didn't mind sweating and getting dirty, and Donny, who would play no matter how hot, cold, or wet it was. Girls were spread all over the place, clustered in twos and threes, sometimes sitting cross-legged on the ground together, a few of them even stretched out on their backs. Lyddy was part of a small gathering that included Kimberly Stafford, and Christine was seated reading at an old picnic table with a few boys who were trying to finish the homework they were supposed to have done the night before.

Everyone had somebody—everyone except for a lone figure that was slowly circling the outside of the playground. I was desperate and decided he was better than nothing.

"My project's ready," I said when I reached Spike. You have to talk about something, right?

"What project?"

"My science fair project. It's this Friday. How's yours?"

Spike made a noise that could have meant anything and started walking again. I followed along rather than just be left by myself.

"So what are you doing?" I asked.

"Looking at everybody. Do you ever wonder what all those girls are talking about when they just stand around together like that?"

He wasn't talking about the science fair, but that was okay. He was talking.

"No."

"I never did, either. But all of a sudden it hit me today . . . what do they find to talk about all the time?"

I looked over at Lyddy and Kimberly. They both

looked incredibly serious. I shrugged. "Current events? Politics?"

Spike looked at me and smiled. "Good. That's very funny, Jasper."

It is always just a little bit creepy when Spike is nice like that.

"Have you finished your science fair project or not?" Spike didn't answer right away, so I decided I'd keep talking. "I have six petri dishes with mold growing on bacteria I collected—from drains and places like that. Then I have one of those big bifold presentation boards. Down at the bottom I have something written about each dish. I'm going to place the dishes on the table right in front of the board so they match up. Then on one section of the top of the board I have this big picture of Alexander Fleming that my father had enlarged at his office. In the second section I describe what a pit his lab was and what kinds of things could have ended up growing in his dishes. And in the last section I have all this research I've done about what life would have been like without penicillin or the antibiotics that have been developed from it because—"

"What are you going to miss about this place next year, Jasper?"

I couldn't believe it. Spike was feeling badly about leaving Teddy E. in a few months? Spike?

"I haven't thought about it," I said. "Next year we'll be

in seventh grade. In seventh grade we go to middle school. That's the way it is. You're going to tell me you think there's something wrong with that, right? You're going to start complaining about having to go to middle school, aren't you?"

"Oh, no. I'm probably the only kid in sixth grade you won't hear complaining about that."

Myself, I was beginning to get kind of excited about middle school. "I heard the seventh grade went on a terrific field trip this past year. And the final exams are so hard they only make you go to school half days while you're taking them. They have all kinds of clubs that meet after school and late buses to bring you home afterward."

"I'm not going to be joining any clubs," Spike laughed bitterly.

"They probably wouldn't have you," I laughed. Then I cringed. How did I ever let that slip out?

"They won't get a chance to decide whether or not they'll have me."

"Oh, come on, Spike," I said, feeling guilty. "Maybe you should join something. There might be something there you'd like. There might be some people there who would . . . like you . . . sort of."

"I'm not going to be joining any clubs, because I'm not going to the middle school next year."

"Sure," I laughed. "Like you have a choice."

"Jasper! I'm not going to the middle school because I'm being kept back!"

"No, you are not."

"Do I have to draw you a picture? The letter came in the mail Saturday. The McNutt's not going to let me leave because she says I'm not ready."

"Ah, she can't keep you from going. Not by herself. Your parents can go to the guidance counselor," I told him. "They can go to Ms. Spendolini."

Spike stopped walking and looked at me. "The guidance counselor and Ms. Spendolini signed the letter."

Ms. Spendolini?

"But . . . but Ms. Spendolini likes you, Spike."

"I thought so."

I shook my head. "You misread the letter."

"So did both my parents."

The bell rang, and we started to walk toward the school.

"This is some kind of mistake. It's one of those paperwork things you're always hearing about on the news," I told him.

"I don't know," Spike said without looking at me.

"Sure. You're Spike Couture. You can't be beaten," I reminded him. "Right? Right?"

He didn't respond. He just stared over the top of the school's flat roof.

I said hello to some kids, got in line, and waited for the teacher on recess duty to tell us we could enter the building. The next thing I remember I wasn't in the hallway heading down to my classroom, which is where I should have been, but running toward the main office.

I started to barge around the counter that separated the secretary's area and the principal's private office from the foyer.

"I have to speak with Ms. Spendolini," I said to one of the secretaries.

"No, you don't," she said without looking away from her computer screen.

"Is she here? She's here, isn't she?"

"She just got back from a meeting at the superintendent's office. She has to return some calls now. You can come in before school tomor—"

"Jasper! Is that you? Come on in and see what came this morning. Look," she said when I entered her office. "Literary magazines."

I ignored the stacks of bound books on her table and the floor underneath it.

"Mrs. McNulty is going to make Spike repeat sixth grade," I gasped. "Why are you letting her?"

Ms. Spendolini looked stunned. "I can't discuss that with you, Jasper. It's a private matter."

"She hates the Cootches, Ms. Spendolini. I know that they're not great students, but they're smart. Anybody can see that. Spike shouldn't have to stay here by himself."

"I'm sorry, Jasper. I've been out all morning, and I have a lot to catch up on now."

"It's not fair that someone who hates him gets to decide whether or not he goes to the middle school."

"Recess is over. You need to get back to your classroom."

"She's just getting back at them for giving her a hard time all year. She's just getting her revenge."

"You don't understand the situation, Jasper."

"No! *You* don't! You wouldn't have signed that letter if you did."

"This is a decision that has nothing to do with you, Jasper," Ms. Spendolini said sternly.

"You're the principal here. You could do something if you wanted to. Why won't you help him? Everyone thinks you're so wonderful! Everyone thinks you're the most beautiful, fantastic person in the building! Why are you letting this happen? Why won't you do something?"

Ms. Spendolini ran to the door to see if anyone was around. Then she closed it partway and stood in front of it.

"I'm letting it happen because Mrs. McNulty is right!"

"How can you say that?" I said. "You don't even like Mrs. McNulty. We all can tell. Why are you helping her?"

Ms. Spendolini turned red. She swallowed a few times and then said, "Mrs. McNulty and I have different ways of doing things. That's all. And just because someone does something differently, it doesn't mean what she does is wrong, you know."

"This is wrong."

"We should not be having this conversation."

"Please help him, Ms. Spendolini. You're the principal. You're Mrs. McNulty's boss. You can stop this."

She walked over to her desk and fiddled with some paper clips she found there. "I can stop it, but I'm not going to." She took a deep breath. "Look, Jasper, I would love to see Spike—and Butch, too—stay just the way he is. People like the Cootches remind us of what we could be if we didn't care about what other people thought of us. We all like to think that we could be free and wild like them if only things were different somehow."

Things would have to be a lot different before I was like the Cootches, but I knew what she meant.

"But that would be so selfish of us," she said gently, "because that's what's best for us and not what's best for them. You are going to grow up and be something very fine. Do you really want Spike not to be able to do that? Do you really want him to stay the way he is just so you can enjoy him?"

I would have to think about that question for a while— maybe a week or two?—before I tried to answer it.

"If Spike hadn't run into problems this year with Mrs.

181

McNulty, he would have run into problems some other year with someone else. Something big has to happen to someone like Spike to make him understand that he has to—"

"Do what he's told?" I asked bitterly. "Be a 'joy to have in class'?"

Ms. Spendolini shuddered. "I don't think he has to go quite that far."

I hoped not.

• • •

"It looks okay," Donny said that afternoon as we approached Spike's house on our bikes.

I was relieved. We had agreed that if there was anything about the house that looked unsafe—say, more than one junk car parked on an unmowed front lawn, boarded-up windows, or barbed wire anywhere—we would turn around and go home. What we found instead was a large, brown, colonial home, one of those types with a rounded, barnlike roof and dormer windows. It had the traditional family room addition and two-car garage. I suspected there was a deck with a grill in back. Though the yard wasn't anything special, there was a row of healthy-looking rhododendrons planted along the front of the house.

Of course, there *were* those picket fences that had been put up along the boundary lines by both the neighbors. But it was only later when I recalled them that they bothered me. At the time, I had other things on my mind.

Donny dropped his bike, eager to be the one to run up to the door on the addition and ring the bell. I don't like to lay my bike down on the ground, so I put up the kick stand and swung my backpack down off my shoulders so I could carry it in my arms.

"He's not here. Are you sure he knew we were coming?" Donny asked.

"I told him before we got on the buses that I'd be here as soon as I could. Try again."

Still nothing happened.

"Keep trying," I ordered as I stepped back on the lawn so I could look up at the windows.

"I don't think he's here, Jasper."

"Ring the bell again. I just saw a curtain move upstairs. Spike!" I yelled. "We know you're in there."

A window flew up, and Butch stuck his head out. "No, he's not."

His mouth was still swollen from the stitches he'd had to have on Saturday, and the words came out, "No, he snot."

The window slammed shut, and Donny leaned on the bell.

"Let us in!" I shouted.

Butch opened the window again. "Spike says for you to go away."

"I thought he wasn't in there," I said.

Butch's head disappeared for a moment. When it reappeared he called, "If he was in here, he'd say for you to go away." Then a look of alarm spread across Butch's face. "Oh-oh," he said just before he disappeared again.

A car had pulled into the driveway. A small woman got out of it.

"I'm sorry, boys, but Spike can't have any guests today," she said as she got out of the car and stood behind its open door.

"Mrs. Couture? My name's Jasper Gordon, and this is Donny Hall. We go to school with Butch and Spike. I sit *between* them."

A look of deep sympathy and then worry spread across Mrs. Couture's face.

"We're here to study with Spike."

Her mouth dropped, and she clutched the car door as if she needed it to keep from falling down. But she recovered quickly. She dived into the car to get her briefcase and the jacket to her suit and then hurried toward us.

"I'll let you in. You know, I've heard the boys speak of both of you. I'm delighted to meet you. Just delighted."

She sounded it, too. She wasn't just talking.

"Spike!" she called as soon as she opened the door. "Spike, you have company!"

Mrs. Couture left the room while continuing to call Spike's name. We took advantage of her absence and openly stared at the furnishings in the family room. There was a woodstove in the corner that had been placed in front of a beautiful wall made of bricks—the real things, not the fake jobs that you glue on. A large-screen TV was surrounded by shelves full of videotapes. The huge coffee table in front of the dark couch was covered with a half-finished jigsaw puzzle. A hard one. All over the room, opened on the furniture or stacked on the floor, were magazines. There were dozens of them (I saw at least three issues of *Seventeen*), looking as if they'd all been half read and then set aside to be picked up and finished later.

Littered across the floor were a couple of pairs of shoes, some dirty socks, a shirt (also dirty), some empty potato-chip bags, and a hairbrush. A vacuum cleaner had been left in front of the sliders that led out onto the deck, signaling someone's good intentions. It looked as if it had been there a long time.

"Could be anybody's house, couldn't it?" Donny whispered.

Not mine, I thought.

"Here he is," Mrs. Couture said as she reentered the room, pulling Spike along behind her. She had large, dark circles under her eyes and looked really nervous. "This is so wonderful. I've often thought that a study group might be just the thing for Spike. He is so full of ideas. They just need to be directed."

That was exactly how Spike looked that moment, as if he had an idea he wanted to direct somewhere. Butch, peering over Spike's shoulder, was less intimidating.

185

"A study group?" he asked. "Is that like homework buddies?"

"Only cooler," I promised.

"It would have to be, wouldn't it?" Spike said as he led us up to his room.

"How come Butch is here?" Donny asked as we started up the stairs. "Your mother said you couldn't have company."

"I'm not company. I've been coming here instead of day care since the beginning of fifth grade. Aunt Evie loves me, and the lady who ran the day-care center didn't," Butch explained.

"She kicked you out, huh?" I guessed.

"My mother says it was all a terrible misunderstanding," Butch said innocently.

"That kind of thing happens to Butch a lot," Spike observed as he stretched out on his unmade bed. A Radio Shack catalogue and the two newest issues of *Newsweek* slid out from between the covers and joined the comics from last Sunday's newspaper on the floor.

Along one wall were two little bookcases at each end of a set of shelves made by propping three boards on some cinder blocks. It didn't look as if Spike was interested in ever finding his books again, just in keeping them up off the floor, which was a whole lot more consideration than he gave his clothing. His dresser drawers looked as if they were never shut, and a cascade of shirts, pants, socks, and some items that I couldn't identify and didn't want to poured from one of them to another and down to the floor. Over by the closet stood a computer stand on which sat a computer, monitor, and keyboard, none of which looked as if they'd been purchased at the same time or maybe even by the same person. Another printer, unattached to anything, sat on the floor. Another monitor had been placed against the wall under the window. Some cords and the ends of two more keyboards stuck out from under the bed. A whole series of pencil or ink drawings I recognized as Butch's work were hung with cellophane tape directly on the Sheetrock of one wall.

I wracked my mind for something nice to say about the mess I found myself standing in and latched onto an electric piano keyboard mounted on a stand at the foot of Spike's bed. "I didn't know you played one of these."

"It's broken," Spike explained. "I'm going to take it apart someday."

As much as I would have liked to have known what Spike hoped to do with used keyboard parts, I stuck to the matter at hand.

"I know you didn't want us to come," I began as I bent down to pull some things out of my backpack.

"I didn't want *you* to come," Spike broke in. "I didn't want Donny to know."

"Didn't want him to know what?" Butch asked.

"Oh, no!" I said to Spike. "You didn't tell me it was a secret."

"What secret?" Butch asked.

"You don't have to worry about me, Spike. I won't tell anybody," Donny promised.

"And I didn't tell anyone else," I said.

"Didn't tell anyone else what?" Butch asked as he looked from me to Donny to Spike.

No one answered him.

"I knew something was wrong, Spike," Butch laughed nervously. "I kept telling you I could tell something was wrong."

"Your parents said nobody could tell you until after school got out because they were afraid you'd pitch a fit," Spike explained.

Butch looked as if he were about to pitch one right then.

Spike rolled over and looked at the wall. "I'm repeating sixth grade next year."

Butch shrieked and covered his mouth with his hands. Then he pulled them down. "I will, too," he announced without hesitation.

"No, Butch. That's not right. You should go on," Spike told him.

"By myself? Not very likely."

"You don't have any say in what happens next year, Butch. Neither one of us does."

"What do you mean we don't? Of course, we do! They can't make me go to the middle school!" Butch started to make a quick breathy noise that was meant to be a laugh. "They can't make us do anything. They've never been able to make us do anything."

Then he started to cry. Just like that, his face was soaked with tears. Donny immediately stepped forward and put an arm around his shoulders. He'd had to comfort a lot of ballplayers in the dugout. I looked away and thought, They're twelve years old. The Cootches are only twelve years old. *I'm* only twelve years old.

"Maybe *Spike* can make *them* do something," I suggested. I had to repeat it to make myself heard over Butch's wailing. Then I said, "He can start working. He . . ."

Spike rolled over and looked at me as if I'd just crawled out from under a rock. "That's the idea you had that was going to help me? That's why you came over here? To tell me to study harder?"

"Well . . . something like that. It's only the first week of May. There's still time. If you work really hard and show everyone you're willing to try, maybe you can convince them to let you go on with us. Show them you can be a good student, Spike, and—"

"And let old McNutty think she's scared me?"

"Yes, Spike! Yes! Do anything!" Butch pleaded.

"Come on, Butch. She'd make me grovel, and then

she'd keep me back anyway. You know she would. She's not going to see me squirm," Spike said, looking determined. "Nobody's going to see me squirm."

"But it's okay for everybody to see you in sixth grade again next year?" I asked.

"That's next year."

"We haven't done anything in class all year long that you couldn't have done if you'd wanted to. Do it now. Donny and I will help you."

Butch used the bottom of his T-shirt to wipe his face. "I'll help you," he sniffed.

"Look." I held up the notebooks I'd brought him. "I've made you a copy of my notes for the next social studies test. And I've shown you how to organize our spelling words so they're easier to remember. Here's—"

Spike knocked them out of my hand. "I don't need help."

He was right. What he needed was a miracle.

"There's nothing McNutty likes better than to force people to do what she wants them to just so she can say she did it," Spike said angrily. "She thought I was going to crawl into school this morning and fill out all her worksheets and copy all her vocabulary words off the board, so she could feel good about how she'd beaten me. Well, I didn't. And I'm not going to."

"I'd like to see somebody beat her at something," Butch said. I could see his teeth clenched on the other side of his puffy lips.

"I'd just like to see somebody embarrass her—in front of a crowd." Donny smiled as if he could picture a scene like that in his mind.

"Who wouldn't like to see something like that?" Spike said. He didn't sound angry anymore. Just sad.

"Is your mother still going to make you do a science fair project?" I asked suddenly.

"I was kind of hoping that my failing sixth grade would put it out of her mind."

"I know you've probably never darkened the door of the science fair, but I can tell you it draws a crowd. A big one."

Butch and Spike looked at each other and grinned.

"Can you imagine the kind of people who go to a science fair?" Butch asked.

Spike actually laughed. "No, Butch, I can't."

"Stay on task, you two!" I ordered.

They both jumped and looked at me.

"It would be pretty embarrassing for a teacher to see a project win, say, honorable mention or third place at the sixth-grade level—if it came from a kid she was flunking."

Butch blew off my idea with a wave of his hand, and Spike said, "That's never going to happen. McNutty controls the science fair."

"Not the judging. Not this year."

Finally, I had said something that attracted a little attention from Spike. But not for long.

"Let's get real," he said. "What are the chances of me—"

"I'll help you," Butch said eagerly.

"What are the chances of the two of us together coming up with a project good enough to get honorable mention?"

"They would be better," I admitted, "if you had someone else to help you."

Spike suspected what I was driving at, but he didn't say anything.

"Someone like me."

"Hah! Like that's going to happen."

"I am telling you, Spike, I can help you get her. I *will* help you get her."

I felt as if there should be a full orchestra playing somewhere over our heads and maybe capes and masks, a hidden fortress . . .

"What do you say?" I asked, my eyes locked with Spike's.

"Urp . . . Sorry. That was me," Butch said as he patted his stomach.

I sighed and bent to pick my notebooks up off the floor.

"Would the project have to be on photosynthesis?" a voice above me asked.

"I guess not," I replied, trying not to sound too hopeful.

"I don't want to do anything on weather, either. Or the ocean. I hate studying the ocean."

I stood up and shrugged casually. "You can do anything you want, Spike."

"Rocks. I particularly don't want to do a project on rocks. I don't like studying stars, or trying to figure out if people will be born with blue eyes or brown, or . . ."

I asked him to wait while I found a pencil. "I'd better start making a list," I said.

Thirteen

After All
These Years

At six-thirty Friday evening, the doors were opened for the Theodore Ervin Elementary School's Eleventh Annual Science Fair. Some parents had been working since one o'clock that afternoon setting up tables and chairs, putting up the kindergarten classes' nature wall hangings, assigning spots to the sixty-four student projects they were expecting, and making up gallons of orange mystery punch. The fair didn't actually begin until seven o'clock, but the students with exhibits came tearing in as soon as Ms. Spendolini unlocked the door to the gym.

The younger kids went nuts as soon as their parents got their projects set up. They ran up one aisle and down the next, stopping every few feet to study a project on color or poke at someone's hamster or ooh and aah over baby chicks that had never made it out of the shell—the ultimate science project gone bad. The other most popular displays were the ones that included food: the earthquake cake, the cookie rock formations, the gumdrop and toothpick demonstration on the strength of triangles as geometric forms.

Personally, I wouldn't dream of sampling something from an exhibit area. I even try to avoid the orange mystery punch, and the parents make that.

My display area was located between Donny's electrical circuit and another boy's tornado in a soda bottle. After politely admiring both projects, I left my father to take care of mine and walked across the aisle to look at Lyddy's.

She was sitting dejectedly beside a display board in the middle of which was a hand-drawn and -colored layout of a human esophagus, liver, stomach, gall bladder, pancreas, small intestine, large intestine, and appendix.

"This is beautiful. I didn't know you could draw anywhere near this well," I said appreciatively.

"Butch did it for me," Lyddy said. "He copied it right out of a book. This project can be duplicated by others—and has—but notice that there's nothing here I've observed, no errors addressed, zip. It's a project that has 'loser' stamped all over it."

"Thanks, Lyddy."

"This plan of yours better work. I hate sitting here knowing I don't have a ghost of a chance of winning anything."

I knew how she felt. I hadn't damaged my dishes of mold and bacteria until an hour before. It was just too painful. I kept hoping I would think of some way to avoid trashing all my months of work. But three days wasn't long to come up with a project that could even win honorable mention for Spike. It was only logical to try to cut out some of the competition, and the only competition I could cut out was Lyddy's and mine.

The science fair was like an open house. We exhibitors sat at our places and received visits from friends, neighbors, and perfect strangers; then we got up and ran around to see what our friends were doing. I tried to get over to the Cootches' project early on, but I could see Mrs. McNulty and the judges already starting to move through the exhibits. I needed to be near my project when they got there in case they had any questions.

Besides, I thought, they *should* be able to set the thing up on a table by themselves.

"This is one of my favorite projects," Mrs. McNulty said when she arrived at my exhibit with the judges, two women in faded blue jeans.

"Oh, yeah?" one of them said without much interest.

"Yes, indeed. Jasper, here, is one of our most outstanding students. A role model, too."

She patted me on the back. I could feel my flesh crawling under her hand.

"I'm sure you'll agree he chose a fine project. Using bacteria to grow mold allowed him to experiment. And then he connected his experiment with the work of one of the giants in the field of—"

"Mold?"

"Bacteriology," Mrs. McNulty snapped.

The three of them hadn't visited even a quarter of the exhibits, and already Mrs. McNulty's patience was wearing thin. The state of her patience didn't seem to bother the women she was with one bit.

One of the judges hadn't spoken at all. Now she said, "What happened to those two cultures right there?"

I looked over at the petri dishes I had stirred up and nearly emptied before leaving home.

"I think a cat may have got into them."

The more talkative woman patted me on the back. "That's too bad. It was a good idea."

They walked away, leaving Mrs. McNulty staring at my project.

"A cat did this?" she asked. "Did I hear you correctly?"

"I left my dishes on the back porch for a little while," I said. And I had. "One of our neighbors has a lot of cats . . ." Which she does. "There's no controlling them, you know. Cats. I think one of them must have come over in our yard. Right up on the porch. That could have been what happened."

I'd seen that look of disbelief on Mrs. McNulty's face many times before. It had never been directed at me, though. If she had said something to me, something like, "How could you do this after I've been so nice to you all year?" or "You must be so disappointed, Jasper, dear. But you and I know it was the finest project here, don't

197

we?" I probably would have caved in and warned her about what was going to happen. I admit it. If she had said or done anything to remind me that I didn't have to fear and hate her because I wasn't Butch or Spike or Donny or Christine or any of the kids she had been mean to and embarrassed, I'm afraid I would have become her secret weapon again.

Instead, she made a messy, snorting noise and said, "Well, I hope you've learned something from this," and hurried off to rejoin the judges.

The three of them hit every exhibit, even the hopeless ones like Lyddy's. It dragged the judging out, and a lot of the smaller children, whose parents had done their projects for them, anyway, and who really didn't know what they were doing there, got bored and started fighting. Ms. Spendolini had time to say hello to every kid in the room. Donny kept drifting over from his area, and Christine came through with her brother. Even Butch finally stopped by with a fistful of doughnut holes.

"Want one?"

I looked down at his greasy hand.

"I'll pass."

"You did a nice job typing out all this stuff and gluing it on your display."

I opened my mouth to make a crack about what kind of lame brain couldn't use scissors and a glue stick. Then I realized he was serious. And Butch did seem to know a thing or two about how to make things look nice on a page, so I just said thanks.

"Ours looks good, too."

"Thanks," I said again. "I'm glad you like the way it turned out."

Butch nodded. "Spike and I fixed it up last night and this afternoon. It's really cool now."

"Wh . . . what?"

"We added a bunch of stuff. It's great now."

"It was great when I left Spike's house yesterday afternoon!" I said. I was so upset my voice cracked.

"It was *good* when you left. Now, it's *great.*"

My project! I thought. My beautiful project! I'd sacrificed it for nothing.

I looked toward the other side of the gym to try to see where their project was being exhibited. "Have the judges been by yet? Maybe there's still time to fix it."

"I'm telling you, Jasper, *we* fixed it."

I started to push and shove my way through the clusters of people blocking the aisles, but I'd only made it to the end of the first row of exhibits when I heard, "Your attention, please! ATTENTION, PLEASE!"

I was too late. Mrs. McNulty was introducing the judges.

"On behalf of Ms. Spendolini and myself I want to thank Mrs. Dijon-Jones from New England Adhesives and Ms. Perkins from Tri-State Disposal Services for judging our event tonight and making this a *very special* evening for all of us. Our students have been preparing for months for their visit, and I think they have planned a lovely selection of high-quality projects. Mrs. Dijon-Jones and Ms. Perkins have made their decisions, and I am going to turn the announcement of the winners over to them."

The crowd greeted the judges with a polite round of applause.

"Thank you, Mrs. McNutty," one of the judges said.

That slip of the tongue brought on another round of applause and a number of snickers from parents, which Mrs. McNulty pretended to ignore. She stood with her hands clasped in front of her, the expression on her face declaring that something important was about to happen.

It stayed there while Mrs. Dijon-Jones gave a nice little speech, which no one believed, about how they had seen dozens of wonderful projects and that each and every child there was a winner. Ms. Perkins, her partner, went on to her talk, which no one understood, about how science was part of every moment of our lives and that they liked to see projects reflect that.

They then began announcing the grade-level winners, starting with kindergarten and working their way through the fifth grade. I was sick, certain that the Cootches had fouled up their project so badly that it wouldn't make honorable mention—which was absolutely all it had any hope of winning. But by the time Ms. Perkins began to introduce the sixth-grade awards, I was beginning to feel hopeful again. After all, I hadn't actually *seen* what they'd be up to.

"There was one project we saw this evening we really feel we want to recognize," she said. "It was specific, it followed a logical procedure that others could duplicate, and it had a human touch."

I took deep breaths, trying to calm myself down. Okay, I told myself. That *could* describe Butch and Spike's project.

"Unfortunately, he ran into a problem with a cat. And while that took him out of consideration for any of the regular prizes, we felt that it illustrated the part luck—bad as well as good—has in research. And given that his project involved one of the luckiest researchers of all time, we thought it was appropriate to award honorable mention to Jasper Gordon for his project, 'Alexander Fleming's Discovery of Penicillin: It Shouldn't Have Happened Like This.'"

My father nudged me out of my chair, and my mother beamed. Donny cheered, and I could feel Lyddy's narrowed eyes tearing at my back as I stumbled by them.

Honorable mention for our grade level? That was supposed to have been Butch and Spike's award, not mine. Honorable mention for our grade level? I'd *never* won an award that low at a science fair before. It didn't even rate a ribbon! Just a lousy certificate! I gave up my chance at the biggest award at the fair, not to bring down Mrs. Mc-Nulty, but to get honorable mention for the sixth grade?

As I shook all the hands I was supposed to shake and went to take my place with the other winners who were clustered together at the front of the gym I felt as if I were walking through a nightmare. I was just thinking how much I wished Freddy Krueger would come by to put me out of my misery when Mrs. McNulty grabbed me by the shoulder and pulled me next to her. That brought me back to reality, but in the process I missed the announcement for the third place winner for our grade. But I know it wasn't Butch and Spike. They didn't take second place, either. And first went to Kimberly Stafford's project on the efficiency of different types of liquid dish-washing detergents.

"And we understand that this is the first time she has ever entered the fair!" Mrs. Dijon-Jones said. "Well done, Kimberly!"

As Kimberly made her way up to the judges, she was followed by this pathetic wail. Afterward, I swore to Lyddy that I was sure I was the only one who knew where it came from, and even I barely noticed it because I was listening to Mrs. McNulty muttering, "Dish-washing detergent—what kind of project is that?"

It was all over. The judges started announcing the winners for the entire fair. I stood up there smiling until I thought my lips were going to start bleeding. And all the time I was thinking, I have failed.

"Our third-place winner, for his project 'Earwax: It's There for a Reason'—Eric Frankes!" Ms. Perkins called out.

At the mention of earwax Mrs. McNulty went rigid beside me. When the kids and dads in the audience began to hoot and holler appreciatively for the second-grade boy who came running out of the crowd, her face became hard and yellow—waxy, in fact. She leaned down to me, got her mouth close to my ear, and whispered, "You couldn't even beat that?"

Ms. Dijon-Jones announced the next award. "In second place for the finest project on lint that I, personally, have ever seen is Ian Janicki!"

The third-grade boy who took the red ribbon indicated to the judge that he'd like to say something. She handed him the microphone.

"My sister, Christine, helped me," he said gratefully. "A boy in her class told her how to do science projects."

"Was that you?" Mrs. McNulty whispered accusingly.

"And now . . ." Mrs. Dijon-Jones paused and grinned out over the crowd.

I closed my eyes. This could have been mine. Everyone said so. I gave my chance away.

". . . our first-place winner . . ."

My prize.

". . . whoops! I mean winners, for their project 'A Survey of Sports Injuries at the Theodore Ervin Elementary School with Particular Focus on and Analysis of Individuals at Risk with Predictors of Future Damage and Impairment,' Butch and Spike Couture!"

It was the weirdest couple of minutes I had ever known. The walls, the roof, even the floor seemed to expand as if the room were taking in a big breath, gasping. Then everything came back into place and an uproar followed that was so wild I had trouble later recalling all that actually happened.

I was aware of Lyddy standing and clapping, looking happy for the first time all evening. I could see my parents applauding enthusiastically. Donny was laughing so hard he stumbled against the table he'd used for his project. Ms. Spendolini was on the other side of the judges, laughing and applauding, too. The Cootches' dads were slapping each other on the back, and Mrs. Couture and a woman I assumed was Spike's aunt were both kissing Butch. They couldn't reach Spike because he was standing on a chair shouting, "Yes! Yes! Yes!" and raising a fist into the air.

"That was supposed to be you!" Mrs. McNulty spit into my ear. Out of my right eye I could see her face contorted in anger. But by the time she straightened up to face the crowd, she had that smile in place, the one we all knew so well.

"Is this great or what?!" Butch kept shouting as he and Spike barged through the crowd.

"It's great! It's great!" I laughed as Butch threw his arms around me.

Spike wasn't hugging anybody. He didn't say anything, either, not until after he had his ribbon in his hand. Then he held it up over his head for everyone to see.

I was weak with relief. It was all I could do to get up on my toes to get a better view of the Cootches' project. I couldn't miss it from where I was standing at the front of the gym. It covered one and a half tables and included a pie chart describing a survey of all the sports injuries that had occurred to students over the past four years, another chart that contained data on injuries per student, a display of photographs and X rays of Butch's injuries as well as a life-size diagram of a human body with red X's marked on it, a poster with pictures of broken bones, and a computer terminal displaying a program with which any person could enter the name of a sport and call up the statistical likelihood of Butch being injured taking part in it at some future time.

"What did you do to it?" I asked.

"Remember how you said a science fair project could be a model, a display, or a survey? Well, we decided to add models and displays to our survey. We figured that would make our project three times as good as everyone else's," Spike explained.

"And we made it all about me so it would be specific," Butch explained.

"I have to admit, though, this is a little more than I expected," Spike said, staring at his ribbon.

It was a lot more than I had expected.

"You like it?" I asked.

"What I liked," Spike said, grinning, "was the look on Mrs. McNutty's face when they announced our names."

"I thought she was going to drop dead!" Butch broke in.

We turned to find Mrs. McNulty looming up behind me. The nasty grin on her face seemed to be flickering as if it were shorting out. I could almost hear the sizzle of circuits going bad.

"What did you DO?" she demanded. "You haven't failed to place in the science fair for the last three years, and you've won the last two. What happened tonight could never have happened without your help. What were you THINKING?"

"I was thinking it was the right thing to do," I said slowly.

"You're not supposed to think," Mrs. McNulty raged. "You're just supposed to do what you're told. Following instructions! How could you forget that? After alphabetical order, it was the most important thing you were to learn this year!"

My parents had come forward to share the big moment. Dad, who always likes to know he can catch in reruns anything he may have missed during an actual event, had his video camera running.

"Maybe you'd understand if—"

"I understand you just ruined the most important competition of your life. You blew your chance. You couldn't

206

even beat a project on lint. You gave your first-place prize to the *Cootches!*"

Adults stood around us gaping, except for the ones who had cameras. They took pictures.

"Hey!" Spike complained. "He didn't give it to us. We won it." He gave me a quick look. "No offense."

"That's right," Butch agreed, sounding very put out. "He couldn't have given his first-place prize to us if we hadn't been here to take it."

Dozens and dozens of people were crowding into that end of the gym to see what was going on. My father had to keep shoving his way back to the head of the pack to keep me in camera range. But Mrs. McNulty didn't have any trouble staying so close I could smell her breath.

"After all these years of never having a thought in your head that I or another teacher didn't put there," she said in a low, menacing voice that slowly grew louder, "why did you choose *my* night to decide to think for yourself?"

She punctuated the "to think for yourself" with shoves against my chest that would have knocked me off my feet if Butch and Spike hadn't been there to catch me.

Very soon after that I found myself posing for pictures with the science fair judges while Mrs. McNulty spent the rest of the evening in a meeting with Ms. Spendolini, my father, and my father's videotape.

• • •

That was the last time any of us would ever see Mrs. McNulty, though Kimberly Stafford would swear that she ran into her working at a post office in another town. She was giving a customer a hard time about the way he'd wrapped a package.

"Brown tape," Kimberly heard her tell the man. "It's the finest mailing tool ever invented."

Fourteen

An Extended Bacteria Metaphor

If we had known we could get rid of Mrs. McNulty just by getting her to hit one of us, we would have done it ages ago. I'm sure Spike or I could have got her to take a swing at us by Thanksgiving," Butch complained.

"See? That's the kind of thing they don't tell you at school," Spike pointed out. He sounded very wise now that he was an elementary school graduate.

It was the first day of summer vacation, and the three of us had ridden our bikes to the Teddy E. parking lot. I thought I would have to make up some kind of excuse for wanting to go there, but as soon as I mentioned the place Butch and Spike shifted gears and took off.

"It's so strange to think of somebody . . . retiring suddenly . . . because of me," I said as I looked up at the window of our sixth-grade classroom. I had tried not to dwell on the details of that situation during the last few weeks of school. It hadn't been easy, but what with our substitute assigning a research paper, studying for final exams, and my Teddy Scholars project on Radioactivity—It's All Around Us, I could go several hours at a clip, even a whole day once, without thinking about how Ms. Spendolini had given Mrs. McNulty a choice of retiring or being fired. But since school had ended at ten after one the day before, thoughts of Mrs. McNulty had been attacking my brain like some kind of disease. "All I wanted to do was embarrass her—maybe get her to let Spike go to the middle school with the rest of us. How could I have known . . ."

Butch and Spike gave each other that look that said they were thinking the same thought, whatever it might be. Then Spike interrupted me. "I get so sick of you always trying to take credit for getting rid of the McNutt. We were on that woman all year long. She shoved you around once or twice, and you suddenly start acting as if *you're* the one who saved mankind from her."

"Yeah," Butch added. "There are generations of Teddy E. students who have yet to be born who owe Spike and me a debt of gratitude."

I felt a smile forming. "Maybe someone should build you guys a statue," I suggested.

Butch laughed this deep, weird laugh that seemed to come from the same place his burps originated. "We should at least get a plaque somewhere on the playground."

They were deep into a discussion of the wording

they'd like to see engraved on their memorial when Butch suddenly pointed to someone getting out of a car and shouted, "Hey! Look over there! It's Ms. Spendolini—in shorts!"

We jumped back on our bikes again and tore off to greet her.

"Lyddy feeling any better?" Ms. Spendolini asked when she saw us.

The week before, Lyddy had won only the Theodore Ervin Memorial Award for Excellence in Math. Kimberly Stafford had been named the Student of the Year and took all the other academic awards except for the one in science, which went to me, and the Rabid Reader Ribbon, which Christine won.

"Oh, yeah. Now that she knows Kimberly Stafford is going away to a private school next year she figures she can take over the middle school," Spike explained. "Maybe you should warn somebody over there about her."

"They're already scared to death there because they've heard you two are coming," Ms. Spendolini said.

I grinned. "They should be scared."

She tried to look stern. "You had a very close call, Spike. It was almost too late to start dazzling us with good grades."

"It *was* a dramatic eleventh-hour victory, wasn't it?" Spike said smugly.

"It was dramatic, but I'd hardly call it a victory. More

like squeaking through," Ms. Spendolini replied. She turned her attention to Butch. "I know you did a lot better this past month, too."

"It wasn't as if I could do much worse," he admitted.

"Keep in touch next year, boys," Ms. Spendolini said before heading across the parking lot toward the school building.

"I'll send you a Christmas card," Spike called after her in a tone of voice that meant he'd do nothing of the kind.

Ms. Spendolini turned around and walked back toward us. "I still send Christmas cards to some of *my* grade school teachers. Really. There are three of them I write to . . . just to let them know I'm not in jail. And I always make sure they know that if they were working in my school, they'd be working for me. Oddly enough," she concluded, "they never write back."

"You had teachers who thought you'd end up in jail!" Butch exclaimed.

"Or worse."

She was still laughing when her eye fell on me. "Jasper, I never had a chance to tell you this, but I agreed with those science fair judges. Your project was good."

I smiled politely. I knew she was just looking for something nice to say to me. I appreciated it. We hadn't exactly had much to say to each other the last six weeks of school. I had to face facts—she had never had much to say to me at all.

"I know that you don't care much for Alexander Fleming and how he did things, but you should try to understand that penicillin wasn't his only contribution to the world. We should always remember *how* he made his discovery. That was important, too. There are always going to be times when things aren't going to go the way we want them to or the way they're supposed to. It doesn't matter how good we are at following instructions and procedures. Sooner or later, we all end up with mold on our bacteria. Some of us are able to recognize that we can make penicillin out of it, and some of us aren't." She looked over at Butch and Spike and then back at me. "Try to be the kind of person who doesn't throw away something valuable because it wasn't supposed to be there."

"Wow, an extended bacteria metaphor," Spike said, his voice full of admiration as we watched her walk away. "And she didn't even look as if she was trying."

"But what does it mean?" Butch wanted to know.

"It means," Spike gloated, "that when you win a science fair and see that it makes your teacher sick, then you know you've found the way to get even with her for every rotten thing she's ever done. Every time that substitute gave me back a paper with an A on it (or a B, for that matter), I thought, This one's for you McNutty! Take that!"

"If only Mrs. McNulty had been here to enjoy it with us," Butch said sadly.

"You wait. There'll be teachers at the middle school who will give us a hard time . . ."

That's for sure, I thought.

". . . and when they do, we're just going to throw a couple of perfect exam papers on their desks and tell them what they can do with them. Doing well is the best revenge."

"We're going to the middle school next year!"

The words just burst out of me, and I was embarrassed because I was afraid I sounded like some kind of wuss, getting all choked up about leaving his little elementary school. Which wasn't at all the case. I wanted to leave Teddy E. and go to the middle school.

Didn't I?

I raced around the almost empty parking lot. I passed the door I used to go through when I was in kindergarten. There was the spot where my mother always left me off on days when she drove me to school. There were the swings I swung on when I was little.

I braked suddenly and balanced myself on the seat of my bike. Except for the swings, which I hadn't been near in years, I really couldn't think of a whole lot I was going to miss.

The Cootches stopped next to me, with Butch halting so abruptly that he lost his balance and keeled over. He wore a particularly large, heavy bicycle helmet, and it made him a little top heavy.

"Ah, it's nothing," he announced as he slowly rose up

off the ground and wiped some blood off his chin and knees.

Spike sucked in his lips in, I'm sorry to say, a pretty lame impression of Mrs. McNulty and boomed, "They don't have playgrounds at the middle school, you know! No recesses, either."

I had recovered by then. "That's okay. Recess was beginning to get old, anyway."

"Oh, I suppose you're happy to have more time for studying, right?" Spike laughed.

"I thought you guys were going to start working hard so you could use your good grades as weapons against the teachers at the middle school," I said.

"Not if it means working more than forty minutes a day, right, Spike?"

"Oh, please, Butch. I figure not more than fifteen or twenty minutes, tops."

Spike's eyes suddenly popped as if something he had been meaning to tell us just happened to float to the surface of his brain right then. "I had a great idea last night! What do you say the three of us take *West Adams Uncensored* on-line next year! I read about a couple of guys who started an on-line magazine for just eighty dollars."

I groaned. "Are you going to try to get me to type and spell-check this thing?"

"Actually, I wanted you in on this so you could help pay for it. But, yeah, sure, you can type, too," Spike agreed.

Butch licked his fingers and ran them across the scrape on his face again. "Look at my lip," he ordered.

"It's all right," I assured him. "You just hit your chin."

"That's not what I mean. Look at my lip. Do you see anything different about it?"

"Like what?" Spike asked suspiciously.

"Like hair! I've got a mustache!"

"It's dirt!" Spike roared.

"It is not! It's there all the time!"

"How long has it been since you washed your face?" Spike wanted to know. "Not that *I* think you should be washing more, of course."

"Butch! You're twelve years old! You don't have a mustache yet," I told him firmly.

"Any fool can see it," Butch complained. "You guys are pretending you don't because you're jealous."

"You don't have a mustache," I repeated.

"But I do see a zit over by your ear," Spike volunteered.

"A zit? Really? Okay! And *I* am the first one to get one!"

"And we *are* jealous," I laughed.

Then I suggested we head over to the park. It was the first time I'd had my bike out of our neighborhood, and I wanted to go everywhere.